**David Marshall** is an award-winning author and i science and discovery adventure stories. His storytelling connects children to their world, their parents, their teachers, and with each other. David's lifelong belief – that children learn to trust, dream, and succeed through reading – guides the rich inspirational messages and vivid illustrations in his work. This inspiration, thoughtfully buoyed by soundly researched science and cultural issues, helps our children confront, understand, and address the challenges they face across our planet every day.

Other books by David Marshall

From Bears and Trees to Mushrooms and Bees

I Learned Something Today

Hiccup - The Boy Who Had Everything

I Just Want To Be Normal, That's All

Finn, The Frog Who Played the Violin

What Will I Become?

Addo, The Story About a Baby African Elephant

What Is Out There Beyond My Branch?

Max and the Spirit Bear
The Last Place On Earth

Storyman Books

http://www.storymanbooks.com

davidstoryman@gmail.com
http://www.storymanbooks.com

Published by Healthy Living Publisishing LLC
http://www.healthylivingpublishing.net

Library Congress Cataloging-in-Publication Data
Marshall, David
Max and the Spirit Bear
The Last Place On Earth
Includes bibliographical references and index.
1. Juvenile Fiction 2. Mushrooms 3. Bears 4. Science/nature/Environment

ISBN 978-0-578-59587-0

Library of Congress Control Number:
Printed in United States of America

First Edition

This book is dedicated to the Spirit Bear and all the wildlife of the Great Bear Rainforest, BC, that gave this author/illustrator a new understanding and respect for this big, beautiful, and delicate planet.

CONTENTS

Foreword

When I was a little boy, I dreamed of two things: playing hockey in the NHL and taking pictures of bears. When I turned six years old, I got my first camera, a little, black Kodak Instamatic, and every trip my family would take, I'd be glued to the car window staring out hoping to spot a bear. I even started to keep a photo album of all of my animal pictures, moose and bighorn sheep, and even tiny, cute black bear cubs!

When I grew up and got older, I decided that I wanted to be a professional wildlife photographer, traveling all around the country taking pictures of bears and other animals and telling their stories to people to get them excited about our wonderful wilderness areas across Canada and the United States.

On one of those journeys, I got on a float plane for the first time and traveled to the Great Bear Rainforest, where I took my first pictures of grizzly bears eating salmon. I loved the rainforest so much that I started to go back every year, sometimes two of three times in a year. And one time, I got on a small boat and I went to a beautiful, forested island in the northern part of the Great Bear Rainforest and saw my very first spirit bear. It was climbing high in a tree eating tiny, sweet, wild crabapples and I was so excited that I almost fell off the boat!

Since that first sighting of a spirit bear, I have gone back every single year and photographed lots of spirit bears, big males like the Boss and Clinger and Warrior, and beautiful sows like Molly and Strawberry and Ma'ah (which means Grandmother in the native Gitga'at language).

I think we are very lucky to have a wild place like the Great Bear Rainforest where these spirit bears live and I hope that this book from David Marshall gets all of you excited about spirit bears and that one day you get to go visit this magical place of towering trees taller than the tallest building and creeks so full of salmon that even the smallest, youngest spirit bear can catch enough salmon to grow up into a big, adult bear.

John E. Marriott
JOHN E. MARRIOTT WILDLIFE AND NATURE PHOTOGRAPHY
http://exposedwithjohnmarriott.com
www.wildernessprints.com

Acknowledgements

For me, growing up always felt like a struggle. How to fit in, trying to figure out the answers to the questions we all ask. Who am I? What is my purpose? For me, I have always had to learn the hard way, and life lessons never came easy.

Books can change your life.
As a small boy, the first book that changed my life was, *Where the Wild Things Are*, by Maurice Sendak. I knew in an instant what I wanted to be when I grew up–a children's book illustrator. The second book that changed my life was, *The Giving Tree*, by Shel Silverstein. I knew in an instant that I wanted to grow up and write children's books.

It would be 48 years before I would even try. That is because it would take 48 years before I would ask myself for the first time the most important question I could ask, what kind of person would I have to become to attract a life partner like her? So, it is to my wife, Becky I thank first and foremost for seeing me and giving me the space to discover who I am. To my sons Reid and Owen, who inspire me to be better than I really am. I want to thank my dear friend Kevin Stickney, who first gave me the advice that I didn't want to hear. He said, "David, pursue illustration, that is where you will leave your mark." It would take 15 years before I would heed his advice. I want to thank my friend Danny Cahil, winner of Biggest Loser, who, by example showed me that we all must face our biggest fears and when we do, life's biggest surprises are waiting for us. He told me to submit my first book to a publisher. And it worked!

If the first step in life is finding who you are, discovering your purpose is the second step. I want to thank a man who has changed my life, Paul Stamets. If you do not know who Paul Stamets (Pablo), is you will by the time you finish this book. He taught me that we all have a responsibility in caring for this planet, that we must at least try and if you are not sure where to begin, start by looking within.

Once in a while, though rarely, a creative force comes along that makes you say to yourself, "I wish I could do that." I have been fortunate enough to have this happen to me several times during this project. The first time is when I discovered John E. Marriott's photography and documentaries. John's photography/film work grabs you by the throat and makes you want to pay attention. Capturing a moment in time is not hard, but it takes a special gift to capture the invisible, the very soul of life. I cannot thank John enough for being gracious enough to open up is photo library to me so that I could use his amazing images as studies for the illustrations in this book.

I mentioned being moved by creative forces more than once during this project. Charlie Russell and Peter James are also photographers gifted with capturing the invisible. Thank you.

This project has taught me that all life is connected and all life has its setbacks and triumphs, whether you are a human being trying to navigate the emotional pathways of life or a small bear cub trying ot live out its life in peace on a remote island in the North Pacific.

To all of you, thank you for enriching my life.

—David Marshall

Paul Stamets is the author of six books, has discovered and named numerous new species of mushrooms, and is the founder of Fungi Perfecti, and Host Defense Mushrooms. He has received many awards, including Invention Ambassador (2015) for the American Association for the Advancement of Science (AAAS), the National Award (2014) from the North American Mycological Association Award (NAMA), and the Gordon & Tina Wasson Award (2015) from the Mycological Society of America (MSA). An avid explorer into the old growth forests, his work focuses on the interconnections of mycelial networks and mushrooms within ecosystems. **http://www.fungi.com**

John E. Marriott is one of Canada's premier professional wildlife and nature photographers, with a career spanning two decades, and images published worldwide by National Geographic, BBC Wildlife, Canadian Geographic, McLean's, and Reader's Digest. He is the wildlife photography columnist for Outdoor Photography Canada magazine. **https://wildernessprints.com**

Charlie Russell is a Canadian naturalist who lived among wild bears in the hopes of proving that they are not aggressive and unpredictable animals.

I spoke to Charlie and explained to him what my project was about, that I wanted his permission to use one of his photographs of the Spirit Bear. Charlie didn't hesitate. He said, "David, this is what it's all about. We share our talents, our passion, and love of nature, and we work together. Feel free use any of my photographs." Charlie passed away on May 7, 2018 in Calgary, Alberta. He was 76.

Kevin Stickney has worked in the environmental communications field for nearly 40 years – the last 20 helping communities and organizations across America and the world manage complex issues related to renewable energy, clean water, air pollution, and land use. An avid conservationist and amateur ornithologist, he believes that informed, inquisitive children hold the key to transformative climate change awareness in our planet. **http://www.calypso.agency**

Peter James doesn't include humans or their infrastructure in his nature work. Though he does have a nautical series which includes boats, the majority of his prints at this time focus entirely on spaces that are undeveloped. He prefers to let nature be the purpose of the work. He hopes his love of these spaces is infectious and "the gallery can act as a kind of hub for nature lovers" in Fairhaven, WA. **https://www.peterjamesphotogallery.com**

To evidence this intention, for every photo James sells, he plants 100 trees through the Trillion Trees Campaign which he cofounded with his wife iMa. Additionally, to offset wood use and impact of the new space, James planted 1,000 trees. **https://www.helpplanttrees.org/**

Introduction

Max continues in this epic adventure visiting his grandfather in the Great Bear Wilderness, a region so remote that humans are the rare species, but bears are not. One particular bear, the Spirit Bear, actually a "black" bear is white and a subject of legend. Only a few have been sighted.

Max's curiosity gets the better of him. He wanders from the safety of his grandfather's cabin, soon to be lost in the wilderness. A chance encounter brings Max and Tonkawa, a young Spirit Bear, together, who has also wandered away from the safety of his home.

Both lost, they find each other. As night descends, they hunker down for the night, knowing their parents must be desperately looking for them. Protecting young from harm is universal amongst parents, bears and humans alike.

Although Tonkawa has been taught to fear humans, and soon Max and Tonkawa find themselves depending upon each other for survival. Max and Tonkawa soon become friends and teach each other cool things that neither knew about.

Soon Tonkawa learns that not all humans are dangerous to their survival. Upon being reunited, and considered naïve, Tonkawa struggles to explain to his bear clan that together – bears and humans - can help protect the Great Bear Wilderness.

But all of that is soon to change when an oil tanker runs around, spilling its toxic oil, threatening the wilderness – its coast lines and the salmon runs the bears depend upon. It seems like the adult bears' fears appear justified.

In a surprising alliance, Max enlists Grandpa's friends in a desperate but heroic attempt to save Great Bear Wilderness from imminent destruction.

This story illustrates that the youngest – children – can teach adults, both bear and human, that our prejudices and fear of each other is not necessary. We hold in common shared interests to help protect the natural environment and ultimately each other.

Minds can be changed.

I hope you enjoy this book as much as I have. I must admit, I was eager to turn the pages, as at times, it is literally a cliff hanger.

Max's adventures will continue in this series, so stay tuned!

Paul Stamets

"Unless someone like you
cares a whole awful lot,
nothing is going to get better.
It's not.

The Lorax
(Dr. Suess)

Chapter One

THE SUMMER BEGINS

"Hey there, Maxie! Boy am I glad to see you!"

"Grandpa!" Max exclaimed as he ran to give Grandpa a big hug.

"It is so good to see you, Grandpa!" Max stepped out of the sea plane and onto the sandy shore of Gribbell Island, an island on the North Coast of British Columbia, Canada.

"Maxie, it's so good to see you! How was your trip?"

"Grandpa, what a trip! First, I had to fly from home to Washington State, and then take a bus up to Vancouver, and from there I flew in a sea plane here. We flew over the mountains, Grandpa! I have never seen anything like it! How did you ever find this place?"

"Well, Max, this is a very special place and people rarely visit here. The only way in or out is by boat or a sea plane."

"Why so remote of a place for a fishing trip, Grandpa?"

"Max, I think you will see that this trip is more than just a fishing trip."

Grandpa smiled. "Let's grab your gear and head up to the cabin, Maxie." He picked up Max's bag and led Max to the car.

After loading the gear into the back of the Jeep, Max jumped into the front seat. They began the hour drive to the cabin.

"So, Maxie, tell me what you learned in school this year. Anything interesting?" This was the one question Max could count on each summer when he visited Grandpa.

"Actually, Grandpa, do you remember Mr. Clark, my science teacher? When I told him I was coming up here with you, he told me how beautiful it would be and he also told me about a bear that only lives here and no other place on Earth."

"He told you about the Spirit Bear?" Grandpa asked, surprised.

"Yes, that's it, the Spirit Bear. He said they are actually a black bear with white fur. He also explained how they are endangered. I asked him if he thought I would see one, and he said that if I did it would be very rare. He said that there are only maybe four hundred to a thousand of them remaining and this is the only place on Earth where they can be found.

"Well, Max, you have an excellent science teacher," Grandpa replied. "I agree with Mr. Clark. I wouldn't count on seeing a Spirit Bear, Maxie, but there are plenty of other amazing things to see here."

As they drove over rocks, rotting logs, and mud, Max began to wonder when they would reach an actual road. "Um, Grandpa?" Max started to ask, when suddenly the Jeep drove over a large rock. The movement lifted him out of his seat and sat him back down hard. "When do you think we will get to a road?"

"Road?" Grandpa started to laugh. "You're on it. Max, there are no roads here because nobody lives here. You may find a few remote campsites, maybe a few rough tracks that could be roads, but most, if not all of those, were abandoned a long time ago. No, Max, we are out here on our own."

Max gripped the roll bar so tightly his knuckles were turning white. He wasn't sure if he was afraid of being the only ones out in this remote part of the world, but he did know that if he was going to be safe anywhere, it was with Grandpa. There was nobody he would rather be with.

As they drove through the roadless forest, navigating over the fallen logs and the moss-covered rocks, Max felt very different in this strange and beautiful world. He has never seen such beauty in his life.

"Grandpa, the trees here look so very different from what I expected."

"This forest is very old. You are in the middle of the lowland old growth rainforest made up of some of the oldest and largest trees on Earth." Grandpa brought the Jeep to a stop and got out. "Max, come with me. I want to show you something."

Max opened his door and climbed out of the Jeep, too. "Where are we going Grandpa?"

"Come, let's walk a bit," Grandpa answered.

"The ground feels like a big sponge," Max said.

"Yes, Max," Grandpa began, "that is because this is a rainforest. The moss grows thick and it grows on everything."

At the base of a giant tree Grandpa and Max stopped and looked up.

"Wow! Grandpa, what kind of tree is this?" Max asked.

"This is one of the most common and oldest trees here, a Western Red Cedar. But that's not all." Pointing as he talked, Grandpa said, "Over there are Sitka Spruce, Western Hemlock, and Douglas Firs. These trees can grow up to three hundred feet tall and some of them have been growing for more than a thousand years."

"A thousand years!" Max exclaimed in disbelief.

"Yes, Max. It all began when glaciers melted," Grandpa explained.

"That was about ten thousand years ago, right?" Max asked.

"Exactly, Max. It sounds like Mr. Clark teaches you a lot of interesting things."

"Oh yes, Grandpa, science is my favorite class and he's the best–my favorite teacher."

Grandpa and Max stood at the base of the giant Red Cedar tree, gazing up into the branches. The tree looked like it went on forever.

"You know why these trees thrive here in this old growth forest, Max?"

"No, Grandpa, why?"

"Because of the salmon. When the Pacific salmon migrates through these waterways, rivers, and inlets, the bears catch them, and eat them. Scavengers like wolves, ravens and other animals take the left-over carcasses into the forest, and these nourish the trees with nutrients, particularly essential minerals from the ocean. They bring them into the forest and eat them among the trees. Then they leave the fish carcasses that are full of nitrogen and they fertilize the soil. Eighty percent of the nitrogen in the forest's trees comes from salmon. This makes the Pacific salmon critical to the health of these forests."

"Wow, Grandpa, that is amazing!"

"Max, there always so much more to learn and understand, but we had better

get to the cabin. It's going to get dark soon."

As they drove the rest of the way to the cabin, Max's head swam from all that he had learned, and that led him to think about his Grandpa. Looking over at his grandfather, Max asked, "Grandpa, how do you know so much about this area and all this science?"

"Well, I imagine for the same reason your science teacher knows a lot, and like you too, Max, I am curious, and I love knowing how things work. I have been studying this area since the end of last smmer, and it has led me to research as much as I can about this rainforest and the ecosystems here. That created an insatiable desire to know more about environmental sciences. When you study how things work, it often gives you insight into creating ways to solve problems."

That was something Max knew about his grandfather very well. Grandpa was always reading and going to the library to look things up. When he couldn't find a certain book or article, he would have the librarian order it. Grandpa never stopped learning.

"You said you've been studying since last summer. Why? What happened at the end of last summer?" Max asked curiously.

"Well, Max, after I dropped you off at the bus station, I headed home, and I was listening to one of my favorite NPR radio shows. They were talking about a Black Bear that is actually white."
"Oh, do you mean the Spirt Bear that Mr. Clark told me about?

"Yes, Max. But it has several names—Kermode Bear, white black bear, and the indigenous people know it as the Spirit Bear. Max, this bear lives in only one place on Earth.

"You mean right here," Max replied, remembering what Mr. Clark had said.

"Yes Max, and actual studies show that there are only roughly four hundred remaining Spirit Bears. They are endangered Max — this whole area is under a lot of pressure. It is a delicate balance of many ecosystems. Even the bears food source is threatened."

"What kind of pressure?" Max asked.

"Well, for example, there are man-made pressures, such as logging companies cutting down parts of this ancient rainforest. The centuries old trees that are critical to wildlife and the ecosystem are in danger from companies that are actively clear cutting, using dynamite to blast large tracks of land, and building roads through Alberta and on Princess Royal Island. These companies are deceiving the public by assuring them that this destruction isn't happening."

"Can't somebody help?"

"Sure, Max! There are many people and organizations who are very concerned — The Rainforest Conservation Society for one. They are one of many organizations working to save this part of British Columbia's heritage."

Max sat quietly as they bounced along the rough ground. "Grandpa," Max asked, "how is it that we can know so much yet care so little?"

"When you study how things work, it often gives you insight into creating new ways to solve problems.

Grandpa

Chapter Two

IT'S A GREEN GREEN WORLD

Tonkawa was born under a moss-covered Hemlock. Taru, Tonkawa's mother, made a nice cozy den in the hollow of the tree. Tonkawa was her first cub.

Taru is a Spirit Bear, one of the last of her kind. When Taru gave birth to Tonkawa, she was so happy to see that he too was a white black bear. Not that she would have loved him any less if had been born a black bear, but because this meant the Spirit Bear, the white colored black bear, just increased their chances for survival. For the rest of the winter months, Tonkawa spent his time snuggling close to his mother, staying healthy by drinking the high fat content of his mother's milk.

As the winter melted away and spring began to warm the air with the sweet smells of moss and evergreens, Taru and Tonkawa left the warmth and safety of their den. It was time for Taru to introduce Tonkawa to the forest and teach him the ways of bears; where to get food, how to fish, and how to sense danger.

As they climbed out from the hollow of their den, Taru noticed something about her baby cub–it was as if he already knew the way of the forest, as if the forest knew how to speak to him.

Tonkawa emerged from his den, and the forest rolled out a carpet of emerald moss, welcoming him to his world.

Under the canopy of the rainforest, lichen dripped from the branches of the Hemlock trees. Taru brought Tonkawa out of their den. Tonkawa will call this magical place home and hopefully live out a long and peaceful life.

Tonkawa looked around and noticed that everything under the canopy of the rainforest looked soft and muted. The ground was spongy, and the air was washed with a bright green as if the spirit of the forest covered everything in a soft carpet of moss. The fog could be so thick that it looked like it was dripping

from the trees. There isn't another environment quite like it in the world.

Rain poured down, covering everything in a shiny film of water. "Mother," Tonkawa asked, "why is everything so wet?"

"This is something you will get used to," his mother replied. "We live in a rainforest. Think of the rainforest as the lungs of the Earth. Rainforests help the Earth to breathe and that is because there are a large number of trees that grow here, perhaps more here than any other rainforest."

"Is that why there are so many plants too, Momma?" Tonkawa asked.

"Yes, Tonkawa, the more rain there is, the more bushes, shrubs, and trees grow. It is the rain that makes everything so lush and green," Taru explained.

She continued, "You will learn that this rainforest is what sustains us, Tonkawa. The plants, leaves, and trees release water into the air, and then the air delivers it back down to the Earth as rain. It's a cycle, and everything is interconnected. As long as the trees are not harmed, the rainforest will thrive."

Tonkawa followed his mother as she led him through the forest, teaching him about the plants. Taru pointed out what was safe to eat and what to avoid.

Tonkawa sat down near a Giant Cedar tree. Taru asked, "You're tired aren't you, Tonkawa?"

"Yes, Momma, a little," Tonkawa replied.

"That's okay. We have walked far enough today. Let's head back home."

"I can walk more, Momma. I just needed to rest." Tonkawa was so excited about his time in the forest exploring with his mother that he didn't want to stop.

"That's enough for today, Tonkawa. You are going to need your rest for tomorrow. It is going to be a big day."

"Why, Momma? What is tomorrow?"

"Tomorrow we are going fishing!"

"Fishing?" Tonkawa had been looking forward to learning how to fish.

"You are in for a real treat! I promise, tomorrow's adventure is one you will never forget."

They walked home through the forest in no particular hurry. Along the way, Taru continued to point out different plants and vegetation, teaching Tonkawa all about the abundance of life that thrived under the canopy of the forest.

Soon they arrived back at their den. Tonkawa walked straight over to his bed, feeling very tired from the adventures of the day.

"That's it, Tonkawa, you go to sleep. Tomorrow we go fishing," Taru said as she tucked him in for the night.

Barely awake, Tonkawa murmured, "Oh boy Momma, fishing!" and then fell fast asleep.

"The one who plants trees, knowing that he will never sit in their shade, has at least started to understand the meaning of life.

Rabindranath Tgore

Chapter Three

IT'S LIKE A TREEHOUSE

"We're here?" Max asked.

"This is it," Grandpa replied. "It's the only cabin for miles. Let's get your gear and I'll show you around."

Max jumped out of the Jeep, excited to be with his Grandpa. "You know Grandpa, it feels like we are the only two out here."

"Well, Max," Grandpa said with a smile, "sometimes you need to be alone in a beautiful place to feel connected to this life. It's one of the best gifts you can give to yourself."

Max grabbed his backpack, thinking how much he loved how Grandpa had a way of explaining things. Turning, he ran up the porch stairs, excited to see the cabin.

Grandpa carried Max's duffle bag and walked in behind Max. Grandpa was happy to have this time with Max.

Max stepped inside the cabin. He looked all around, taking in its rustic, almost abandoned feel. Sitting in the corner of the front room was an old wood burning stove that looked like it had grown out of the floor. To his right, he noticed a ladder.

"Where does that go?" Max asked.

"That goes to your room. Go climb up," Grandpa replied.

Max climbed the ladder. At the top of it, he was up as high as the ceiling.

"This is where I sleep, really?" Max loved it! It felt just like his treehouse back home. "This is so cool, Grandpa!"

"I hope you don't sleep walk, Maxie—that first step will certainly wake you up!" Grandpa said with his dry sense of humor. They both had a good laugh.

"Here ya go, Maxie." Grandpa tossed up Max's duffle bag. "We don't have a lot of room, so it's important we pick up after ourselves. This cabin can get crowded quickly, so we need to make sure we keep it tidy and help each other."

"When it comes to dreams,
do not wait;
the time will never be just
right. Start where you stand,
and work with whatever
tools you may have
at your command, and better
tools will be found
as you go along.

George Herbert

Chapter Four

GETTING LOST IN THE BEAUTY OF IT ALL

Max was anxious to explore. "Grandpa, is it okay if I go explore the cabin and check out the river?"

"Sure, Max. Just be sure to keep the cabin in sight. It's really easy to get lost out here when you don't know where you are. Be sure to take your rain parka since it rains most of the time. Remember, you are in one of the oldest rainforests in the world."

Max was excited. He couldn't wait to explore. He put on his rain parka, tied up his boots, and ran out the door. Standing on the porch, he closed his eyes and breathed deeply, filling his lungs and his head with the fresh smell of cedar, moss, and dirt—a unique smell that only an old growth forest can give.

Max splashed his way across the stream. It was alive with life and bordered by ferns, moss-covered rocks, and rotting logs covered with wild mushrooms. The mushrooms reached up through the rocks in one last attempt at survival. The air smelled of dew and mud. Max loved the way nature seemed to know exactly where to place all the stuff of the forest. All the ecosystems worked together like an orchestra of a thousand instruments. At first look, he wondered how all the instruments could produce anything but a chaotic noise. Max thought there was nothing more beautiful than when everything works in its naturally designed purpose.

Max continued to walk further down the stream, taking in the sights and sounds around him. How fascinating the many shades of green, the translucent emerald moss, Max observed. He loved this magical forest. Out here, deep in the forest, there was a sense of understanding, an unforgiving patience. The forest seemed to forgive through neglect, as if resilient to the clear cutting of trees and relentless grasp at oil from deep in the Earth. But nature also sends warnings.

Max sat on a rock under a large Cedar tree by the river, and through the silence he could hear the light crackling of leaves and a gentle breaking of twigs. Something was walking on the forest floor and getting closer. He turned to look back towards the cabin, but it was nowhere to be seen! He had wandered too far. He sat frozen, waiting for whatever was in the woods to appear.

As he watched, a small white bear cub walked down to the river, taking every step with curiosity, sniffing the air and then the ground. Instinctively, the bear lifted his head to sniff the smells carried on the wind. It was beautiful, and Max wasn't afraid at all.

Max looked up as it started to rain. The water came down hard and washed over everything, but its intensity didn't take away from the magic of this moment in the forest. Max thought that the forest was beautiful because of it. He watched the little bear cub, thinking of how magnificent he was. Max stood in awe of the beauty of this Spirit Bear cub.

I can't believe this place is here on Earth. It's hard to believe this is our home. It's harder still to imagine I am here, Max thought to himself.

"The whole world is a series of miracles, but we're so used to them we call them ordinary things.

Hans Christian Andersen

Chapter Five

AN UNLIKELY FRIENDSHIP

When Taru woke up, Tonkawa was nowhere to be found! Taru began to panic.

"Tonkawa!" Taru yelled out. *Where could he have gone off to?* she wondered.

Tonkawa had never been out so far, so late, and so alone. Being lost wasn't something he ever experienced, and he didn't like the feeling of being scared. He could tell it was getting late because the shadows from the trees were getting longer and that meant night was coming.

"Momma!" Tonkawa called out, but no answer came. As he walked further, he came to a stream, where he saw a human boy sitting alone on a rock. Tonkawa, sitting down quietly, watched the boy for a long time. He had never seen a human before, but he had heard a lot of stories from the elders. Particularly from his uncle Koda, the leader of his family bear clan. Each story ended the same way: "Stay away from humans, they are dangerous and unpredictable."

As Tonkawa watched the little boy on the rock, he didn't feel any danger or fear. Actually, Tonkawa thought, the human boy seemed harmless and gentle. Tonkawa continued to drink from the river, watching the boy at the same time.

The boy was playing with something in his hands. Tonkawa continued to watch with growing curiosity. The boy suddenly slid down off his rock and walked over to the stream, and bending down, he let something go into the running water.

Tonkawa, downstream behind a rotting log, watched as the current carried the object toward him. Tonkawa stayed low because he could see the boy was watching the object float downstream and he didn't want to be seen.

The object turned and spun in the currents whirling pools. When it was in front of him a branch laying in the water snagged the object in front of Tonkawa!

Tonkawa stood up slowly, and began to walk out into the stream to where the object was stuck.

Max stood frozen. Seeing Tonkawa, he sat perfectly still and watched the bear cub. He had only heard about white bears from his grandfather, but he didn't think he would ever see one.

Tonkawa could see that the object was a sailboat made from a single leaf. It looked just the boats he would see from the cliffs when he sat with his mother overlooking the inlet waterways.

This is what the boy had been making, Tonkawa realized. He sniffed the boat, and as his nose touched the boat, it was just enough to set it free from the branch. Once again, it journeyed down the stream.

"Thank you!" came the voice from up stream.

Tonkawa tuned his head and was shocked to see the boy walking towards him.

"You're welcome," Tonkawa said hesitantly.

Max stared at Tonkawa, thinking that the white bear was more beautiful than he could have imagined. Now standing only a few feet away, they looked at each other. Max began to smile and held out his hand.

Tonkawa felt strangely calm, not the panic he assumed he would feel if he ever met a human. But then again, this human wasn't doing any of the things that were described to him. He wasn't unpredictable, he wasn't trying to get closer, and nor did he run away.

Tonkawa thought to himself, *how could a human who made such a wonderful sailboat from leaves be dangerous? No, this human boy is different.*

Max held out his hand and said, "Hi, my name is Max. I am a friend. Don't worry, I would never hurt you." It was as if Max knew exactly what to say.

As they stood in the stream looking at each other, Max asked, "What is your name?"

"My name is Tonkawa." They started to walk towards each other. Tonkawa felt he could trust Max. Sensing no fear in Max, he felt no fear of him. "That was a really cool sailboat you made, Max."

"That was a really cool sailboat you made, Max."

"Thank you, Tonkawa. My grandfather taught me how to make them."

"I have an uncle and he has taught me many things," Tonkawa replied, "but never how to make a sailboat."

"I'm sure he has taught you many things more important than building sailboats out of leaves." Max replied. It was at that moment Tonkawa and Max became friends.

For the rest of the afternoon, they sat by the stream talking. They got so caught up in talking to each other they hadn't noticed it stopped raining, and it was now getting dark.

"Don't you need to get back to your home, Tonkawa? Won't your mother be wondering where you are?" Max asked.

Tonkawa was having so much fun talking with his new friend that he forgot he was even lost.

"Oh yes!" Tonkawa exclaimed. "I'm sure momma is very worried right now. I've never been out this late or alone before, but I got lost and couldn't find my way back."

"Well," Max began, "There's not much we can do in the dark. Why don't I stay with you, and tomorrow morning, bright and early, I'll help you find your way back to your mother." Max didn't want to say it, but he had lost sight of the cabin in the woods. He wasn't sure he could find his way back either.

"Oh, would you Max? That would be great!"

Max knew he didn't have a choice, but he felt bad, knowing how worried Grandpa would be.

As they laid there looking up at the stars, on a soft bed of moss, Max worried about Grandpa, and Tonkawa thought about his mother as they fell asleep. Taru had been looking for Tonkawa for hours and now it was getting dark. She was worried sick.

Where could he have gone? He has never been out in the forest alone before and he has never been out in the forest at night. He must be frightened, Taru thought.

"TONKAWA!" Taru called out, "TONKAWA! My dear boy, where have you gone?"

"Tonkawa, when you appreciate the life you've been given, you understand your connectedness to the life around you.

Taru

Chapter Six

THE GENTLE POWER OF BEING

Taru walked through the forest; the daylight was fading quickly. Taru knew she would have to stop looking and wait until morning to start again.

She found a soft bed of moss under a giant Hemlock tree. She laid there looking up to the stars, thinking about Tonkawa.

"HOO... what are you doing out here in the dark?" came a voice from the branch above Taru's head.

Startled, Taru looked up and saw an owl perched on a branch.

"Oh, it's just you, Owl," Taru said.

"Yes, just me," Owl replied.

"I'm sorry, I didn't mean to offend you. It's just that my cub has gone missing, and I am very worried." Taru replied.

"Oh, no offense taken, Taru. I understand," Owl said with familiarity.

"How do you know my name, Owl?" Taru replied, confused.

"All the creatures know your name. We know the names of all the Spirit Bears on this island."

"Why is that?" Taru asked.

"Because it is the Spirit Bear that keeps us safe and has for thousands of years," Owl explained. "First Nations never speak of you to outsiders — they keep your existence a guarded secret, so very few outsiders know of you. You have

become legend. The existence of the Spirit Bear is the stuff of folklore, of myth."

"And how does this keep everyone safe?" Taru asked, still confused.

Owl continued, "What humans can't see they generally don't believe exists. You are protected, Taru, and let's face it, you and your kind are pretty good at staying out of sight. First Nations believe the Spirit Bear will bring power to those it appears to. They hold you sacred, and to protect you they never speak of you in public. To this day, the people of the Great Bear Rainforest stand guard and watch out for all bears. No hunters come, no trappers, and no thoughtless trophy hunters. We have lived in peace because of you and your kind, Taru.

Taru replied, "I think when you appreciate the life inside of you, you understand your connectedness to all life around you."

"I'm afraid times have changed. Many humans find nothing sacred about these old growth forests or the life that relies on them, anymore," Owl replied.

With concern in her voice, Taru asked, "What do you mean, Owl?"

Owl realized that Taru and most of the bears weren't aware of the threat humans had become. He continued to explain, "The humans are coming with large machines that scrape and dig deep into the Earth. They are laying down long tubes over the forest floor that stretch for miles, clear cutting trees and old growth forests as they go. Trees that have been growing for hundreds of years. They are destroying the delicate balance of many ecosystems."

Concerned, Taru thought about this. Then, looking up to the branch, she saw

that Owl had gone as quietly as he came. An owl can fly in silence—they are the only raptors that can. When Owl took flight, Taru never heard a sound. Talking with Owl took Taru's mind off her cub. Now that Owl was gone, Taru's thoughts returned to Tonkawa and how desperate she was to find him. Lying down on the soft ground of the tall dense forest, Taru looked up into the night sky. Concerned for her cub, she couldn't help but be in awe of the beauty of the world. She wondered what world will Tonawa live in when he has grown up and on is his own? She thought, what will the world be like for him?"

"In nature, nothing is perfect and everything is perfect.

Alice Walker

Chapter Seven

WHEN WE LOOK WE RARELY SEE

Early the next morning when they woke up, Tonkawa noticed a new sailboat made out of leaves lying beside him.

"You made this for me, Max?" Tonkawa asked.

"Yes! Last night I couldn't sleep, so I made you a sailboat. Do you like it?" Max asked.

"I love it! Nobody has ever made me anything before, Max. Thank you!"

They walked down to the river to try out the sailboat. As they watched it dance in the pools of water around the rocks, they heard a loud crunching of leaves and the heavy snap of breaking sticks coming from just inside the forest's edge. With leaves and sticks flying everywhere, Taru came bursting from the forest!

"Tonkawa! Get away from that human!" Taru yelled angrily and with fear! She moved like the wind across the stream; she was upon them in an instant. Standing up on her hind legs, she let out a mighty roar!

Max had never been so afraid. Looking up at Taru, Max closed his eyes. Max thought she must be ten feet tall!

As Taru towered above Max, Tonkawa stood between Max and his mother and cried, "No Momma! This is Max! He's is my friend!"

"Get back Tonkawa, now! This is a human! What have we taught you about humans?"

"I know Momma, but Max is not like those humans. Listen to me! I got lost yesterday and Max stayed with me all night. He was going to help me get home. Here, look, he made me this—he makes sailboats from fallen leaves."

Taru looked back and forth from Max to Tonkawa again. "He makes what from what?" she asked, still not convinced, but definitely curious.

"Sailboats from leaves and they can float on the river. I told him about the boats you and I watch from the cliffs," Tonkawa explained.

"Well, he does seem like a nice boy, I guess…" Taru muttered. Then she said, "Okay, Tonkawa, you two have some explaining to do." Taru dropped back down and sat in front of Max and Tonkawa.

"I was out exploring Momma, you know, like I do. I was so caught up in it that I got lost and I couldn't find my way back. I came to this stream and Max was sitting on the rock over there making a sailboat from leaves." Tonkawa pointed to the rock where he first saw Max.

Taru glanced over at Max and said, "Go on Tonkawa."

Tonkawa looked at Max. "Well, Max and I talked until it was dark and when I told him I was lost he said it was too dark to try and find our way back and that it would be safer to sleep here for the night. He said he would stay with me and help me find you in the morning."

"You did that?" Taru asked, looking at Max. "You stayed with my son all night?"

"Yes, ma'am," Max replied. "To tell you the truth, I am lost too, but I didn't think it would do any good to worry Tonkawa any more than he was. I figured we could help each other."

"Very kind, Max. So, you're lost too?" Tonkawa asked. "Your mother must be very worried."

"Oh, I'm not here with my mother. My grandfather and I are here together. I spend every summer with him. This year he wanted to come here to teach me how to fish. When I got here he told me about you, well, about the Spirit Bears and how you only live here. He said I would probably never see one," Max explained.

"What else did he tell you about us, Max?" Taru asked, curious to find out why his grandfather knew so much about them.

"He said that there are not many Spirit Bears left in the world, maybe four hundred, maybe less."

"Sounds like your grandfather knows quite a lot."

"Oh yes," Max said. "My grandfather is really good at solving problems, too. Last summer, he and I helped save the honey bee from disappearing. Everyone comes to see Grandpa when they have a problem they can't solve."

"Your grandfather seems like a very wise man. You know, Tonkawa has an uncle named Koda, and all the bears come to him when they have a problem too. Your grandfather and Koda sound a lot alike. I guess you will now be able to tell your grandfather that you saw us," Taru replied. They all laughed.

"So, Max," Taru continued, "if you're lost too, do you have any idea which direction your grandfather is?"

Max replied. "I only know I followed the river until I found a stream that was

feeding into it, and then I followed that. I forgot my compass, and Grandpa is going to be so mad, too. He always says, 'Never go out into the forest without your compass,' but that is exactly what I did."

"Well, you boys must be hungry. Let's eat breakfast and then Tonkawa and I will help you find your grandfather. Sound okay to you, Max?" Taru asked reassuringly.

"Eat breakfast? Where?" Max asked. He looked around, but didn't see anything to eat. Suddenly, Taru put her head undfer the water and came up wiht a large salmon in her mouth.

Tonkawa and his mother laughed. Then, Tonkawa took off like a shot, jumping across the river and leaping into a pool. He disappeared under the water. Completely surprised by what Tonkawa was doing, Max ran toward the river to see where he went. Just then, Tonkawa popped up from the pool with a big salmon in his mouth.

"Where did you learn to do that?" Max asked.

"He surprised me too, Max! He must have been watching the other bears much more closely than I realized," Taru replied, feeling very proud of her cub.

"Max!" Tonkawa yelled. "Come on and see if you can catch one!"

Max looked at Taru then back at Tonkawa, and then took off running. He pulled off his shirt and sneakers and dove into the pool where Tonkawa was standing, disappearing into the clear, cold water. Max suddenly popped up from the under water, "Hey, I can't catch any fish!" Taru and Tonkawa rolled on their backs with laughter at the sight of Max thinking he could a salmon in his mouth.

"Well, Max," Taru began, "you can tell your grandfather you learned how not to fish!" And they all laughed.

"I don't know, Tonkawa, this isn't exactly what I expected for breakfast." Max offered the salmon to Taru as he wasn't too fond of raw fish.

"You have to eat something," Tonkawa said.

Taru knew something Max would love to eat. She showed him a bush covered in berries.

After filling themselves with all the fish and all berries they could eat, they laid down beneath the hemlock and spruce trees on a bed of spongy soft moss. Looking up at the blue sky through the leaves, Taru and Tonkawa fell asleep.

While laying down and looking up through the tree canopy, Max thought about his new friends and how Taru and Tonkawa didn't seem too concerned with anything. They seemed completely at peace.

The floor of the forest was a soft carpet of moss, decaying leaves, rotting wood, ferns shooting up from the ground growing randomly, and with purpose. Max had never seen the forest this way before.

Suddenly there came a sound through the trees. Low, gentle, echoing, and drawing closer. The sound seemed to last forever. It wasn't just the crackling of leaves and sticks that got Max's attention, it was more. It sounded like wind blowing through tall grass. Max looked over at Taru and Tonkawa; they were sound asleep.

"Somewhere, something incredible is waiting to be known.

Carl Sagan

Chapter Eight

IT'S IN THE MOMENT OF OUR DECISIONS

He squinted at the tree line at the edge of the river as three bears walked out, pushing through the branches—one black bear cub and two large black bear adults. Max sat quietly, watching the bears walk down to the river to join the other bears drinking, and fishing in the river.

The largest of the black bears raised his head, and with his nose in the air, he glanced over towards Max. Max froze as the big bear started walking towards him. Taru and Tonkawa were still fast asleep.

The large male could see that Taru and Tonkawa were sleeping. He walked right up to Max, and sat down about two feet away from him. He began to speak.

"Hello, human." This huge bear had a low, deep voice, and Max knew instantly who he was: Tonkawa's grandfather. "I am Koda."

"Pleased to meet you, Koda. My name is Max."

"Oh, I know who you are. I have known of you since you landed down on the beach. I have also been watching you from the moment you first walked down to the river from your cabin. Tell me human, why are you here?"

Feeling scared and nervous, Max answered, "My grandfather wanted to teach me how to fish and so he planned our summer vacation here in Great Bear Rainforest."

"Why here, human?"

"He said that we would be the only people here and that this is a very special place."

Koda glanced at Tonkawa sleeping. "Yes, it is. I understand you and Tonkawa have become close."

"Yes sir, we have become very good friends."

"Friends you say?" Koda asked curiously. "Do you know what it means to be called friend?"

Max paused for a moment, thinking his question odd. He had never truly thought about it before, but before he could answer, Koda began, "A friend is someone you are connected to, even when you can no longer share the same time and space. A friend stands guard, watching out for you. A true friend makes you feel good about yourself when you are around them and they make you want to be more than you are. Do you think you actually make Tonkawa feel this way, human?"

"I do not know, Koda, but I do know he makes me feel that way." Max replied.

As Koda spoke, Max was taken back by how deep and powerful Koda's voice was. He could feel it vibrate deep in his own chest.

"But," Koda continued, "you are a human, and we have a code out here that we must live by. I'm afraid Tonkawa cannot be your friend."

Max was startled by what Koda was saying. "What do you mean?

Taru awoke, hearing Max raise his voice. Startled to see Koda sitting with Max, she quickly sat up.

"Koda, why, umm, hello. What are you doing here?" Taru asked, trying to act as if nothing was wrong.

Koda looked at Taru. "What am I doing here? This is our home, Taru, remember?

"Oh, yes, of course, of course. I mean how did you find us?" Taru replied.

"Find you? You're with a human. How could I avoid you?" Koda replied.

"Yes, of course Koda, I understand." Taru seemed worried she had upset Koda.

"I was telling Max here that we live by a code in the forest. I was explaining how Tonkawa cannot be his friend. But you know that already don't you, Taru? And I am sure you have explained this to Tonkawa, haven't you? I mean, you of all of bears should know very well why!"

"I am referring to my son, Hotah," Koda explained to Max in a grave tone of voice, "Tonkawa's father. Hotah was a large white black bear. Early one fall morning, Hotah and I were fishing off the island, just far enough away from the protection of the forest. Hotah didn't see the hunters in their camouflaged boat. By the time I tried to warn Hotah, it was too late; the hunter fired his gun and Hotah fell into the water."

Taru had not explained this to Tonkawa; she was waiting for the right time. Taru looked over at Tonkawa, thinking of when she first found him with Max and how happy he was with him. Max wasn't like the humans they had been warned about.

"Koda, Max is not like other humans! Tonkawa has been so happy being friends with Max, it didn't seem to matter," Taru explained.

"DIDN'T SEEM TO MATTER!" Koda was furious. "You know full well what happens when humans get involved! You know how unpredictable they are! How dangerous they are!"

"Yes, Koda," Taru replied calmly, "I do know very well how some of them are, but this boy is not like them. He would never do anything to harm Tonkawa or any of us."

"You cannot know that, Taru! You can't possibly know that."

By now Tonkawa had been woken up by the loud voices. As he opened his eyes, all he heard was, "Tonkawa cannot be your friend!" He immediately joined in the argument.

"What? Tonkawa yelled, "What do you mean? Max is my friend! He would never do anything to hurt us! Look, he made me this sailboat."

As Tonkawa held out his paw to show Koda his sailboat, Koda swiped at the sailboat and then stomped on it with his huge paw.

"No!" Tonkawa screamed. "You can't do that! Why did you do that?"

Taru's eyes widened as she held her breath. Nobody talked to an elder that way, especially to Koda. Koda bent his large head down and placed his nose on top of Tonkawa's, his eyes narrowing. "What did you say to me?"

Without hesitation, Tonkawa repeated, "Max is my friend and you have no right to tell me I can't be his friend."

Koda's eyes grew red with rage as Taru moved forward and pulled Tonkawa back with her paw. "Now Koda, you know how cubs can be." Taru knew that talking to Koda that way could get Tonkawa very hurt, or worse.

By now the other bears on the river started to gather around. Max, noticing all the other bears, realized that he was in a very dangerous situation.

Max looked back and forth between the three bears, wide-eyed and scared at the sight of these two huge bears arguing. Now Tonkawa was in the middle. Max was surprised at the disrespect Tonkawa was showing Koda. There was no way of telling what Koda would do next.

"Taru!" Koda roared. "You know what I could do to that cub of yours!"

"Yes, Koda, I know very well, but please, I am begging you, he's just a young cub. He hasn't learned all the ways of our bear society yet," Taru begged.

Max had learned in school that bear clans each had an alpha male as their leader. The alpha male's main job was to protect the clan, and nobody would argue with the decisions of the alpha bear. Koda probably weighed about 800 pounds, but when he leaped from a sitting position and stood over Tonkawa, he moved like lightning.

"Tonkawa," Koda began. "In life you must make decisions, and once you make those decisions you must live with the consequences. Do you know the punishment for going against our code and befriending a human?"

Tonkawa was so angry he didn't care. "No, I do not know the punishment for going against the code for befriending a human."

"Banishment, Tonkawa. You will be banished from the clan and forced to wander and survive on your own in the forest."

"Good!" Tonkawa said defiantly.
"Hold on," Max interjected. He couldn't let this happen to his friend.

"Tonkawa, you must listen to Koda."

Tonkawa's eyes widened as his head snapped towards Max. "What? You agree with this?"

"Tonkawa, it doesn't matter if I agree. It's not my place to judge your customs and rules, and I don't want you to lose your family."

75

"I would listen to the human, Tonkawa," Koda advised.

Frustrated, Tonkawa replied, "The code is stupid, and I don't care! You are my friend, Max. You are not like other humans!"

"Tonkawa, you must listen to Koda. He knows what's best," Max pleaded.

"How is that, Max?" Tonkawa began, looking at Koda and the rest of the bears. "How are we and humans ever going to learn to live together if we don't first learn that we need one another?"

"We don't need humans!" Koda said furiously, "I am at the end of my patience with you Tonkawa! You must decide! Either us or Max!"

Tonkawa didn't want to hurt his mother, but deep inside he felt he was right. Looking at Koda, Tonkawa stated, "I understand there are generations of rules and codes we live by, and I understand those rules were put in place to protect us from humans, but all I can say is the old ways won't protect us anymore. If all humans were so bad, then how did I come to be friends with Max? How did my mother change her mind about humans? By getting to know Max. By giving Max a chance, that's how. Fine! I choose my friendship with Max." Tonkawa stood with the certainty of his decision.

"So be it," Koda stated. "I hereby banish you, Tonkawa, from the bear clan. You are to leave and wander the forest alone. Now, the code calls for each bear to turn their back on you until you have left our sight."

All the bears except Taru turned their backs as Tonkawa started to walk into the thick darkness of the forest.

"Taru," Koda said firmly. With tears in her eyes, Taru turned away.

Tonkawa's eyes filled with tears as he turned and walked into the forest. Max didn't know what to do. He couldn't believe what just happened. All he knew was that he had to go with Tonkawa. Walking to the edge of the forest, Max turned one last time to see that all the bears still had their backs turned, but just as he was about to turn and walk into the forest, Taru turned her head. Looking over her shoulder with her eyes full of tears, she blinked them slowly. Max felt the meaning in her eyes. He knew Taru was asking him to watch out for Tonkawa. Max nodded his head reassuringly. He turned to run and catch up with Tonkawa.

"How are we and humans ever going to learn to live together if we don't first learn that we need one another?

Tonkawa

Chapter Nine

SOMETHING VERY BAD IS COMING

Tonkawa had no idea what it would mean to wander such a large, and vast wilderness as the 52,000 acres of Gribbell Island. He walked slowly with his head down, thinking about what had just happened. Max came up beside him and put his hand on Tonkawa's shoulder.

"Max, I couldn't allow them to tell us we can't be friends! I think Koda feeling as he does about humans is a big mistake. And my mother, she must be so upset. What have I done?"

"Do not worry Tonkawa. Koda will calm down and see that he was too harsh."

"Not likely, Max. You don't know Koda. He is a bear of honor and he means what he says."

As they walked, they came onto an overhang, looking out over the waterways below. These rivers and channels wound their way around the Great Bear Rainforest.

While they sat looking at the view, Taru came through the bushes.

"Momma!" Tonkawa ran to her and they gave each other a big hug. "Momma, I am so sorry for the way I behaved."

Taru began to explain. "Tonkawa, you stood up for what you believe, and for that you have nothing to be sorry for. Now, I could be in big trouble with Koda if he catches us together. Let's sit down—we have a lot to talk about. For example, Max is still lost, and his grandfather must be very worried by now. I owe it to Max to help him get back to his grandfather safely. After all, it was Max who kept you safe, Tonkawa."

As they sat overlooking the waterways, a tanker appeared out of nowhere, the kind used for transporting large quantities of oil, diesel fuel, and other hydrocarbons. Tonkawa noticed it was drifting too close to the rocky shore. As they watched, it became clear that the tanker had lost power, and couldn't control where it was going. With horror, Max, Tonkawa, and Taru watched as it drew closer and closer to the rocks.

Max asked, "Why are tankers allowed on these channels? There is no reason for them to use this channel!"

Taru and Tonkawa watched as their hearts sank in despair.

Suddenly, the tankers bow rose up out of the water as if some invisible force was pushing it up, and then it slammed back down hard.

"Look, it must have run up onto to some rocks or a sand bar!" Max said, pointing.

As they watched, a black ooze began to spread along the waterline of the ship and bled out into the waterway. Suddenly, there was a lot of commotion on the deck of the tanker. Life rafts were lowered into the water, and the crew was lowered into them.

Max saw that Tonkawa was frightened and said, "Don't worry, it's going to be okay."

"How? How is it going to be okay Max?" Tonkawa said as he leaned on Max, hiding his eyes into his shoulder. He could feel despair welling up inside him. The oil would ruin everything and how an oil spill could kill all the fish. Then there wouldn't be any food for the bears.

"Max," Taru said, "this is bad, very bad."

"Come with me, I know someone who will know what to do," Max exclaimed, leaping to his feet.

"You do?" asked Tonkawa with hope in his eyes.

"Follow me, we have to hurry!" Max said urgently.

Taru and Tonkawa got up and began to follow Max. The tanker below floated on its side, oil spilling out into the inlet like an alien lost in a world where it didn't belong.

Tonkawa and Taru felt sick. They were afraid that this oil spill could destroy their home and many ecosystems that depend on the maze of channels and fjords. Even the Humpback whales that fed on krill in the deep waters of Gitga'at territory of the Great Bear Rainforest could lose their food source.

The Humpback whales that feed on krill in the deep waters of Gitga'at territory of the Great Bear Rainforest could lose their food source.

"Come, we need to go quickly," repeated Max.

As they ran through the woods Tonkawa yelled, "Max, where are we going? You don't even know where you are!"

Panicked in the emergency at hand, Max had forgotten he was lost. He stopped running, realizing Tonkawa was right.

"Not to worry boys, I know where that cabin is," Taru said. "Follow me."

Both Max and Tonkawa looked at Taru with surprise.

"You do?" Max asked.

Smiling, Taru said, "Of course! I know this forest like the back of my paw."

"So, Max, why are we going to the cabin?" Tonkawa asked.

"To see my grandfather! He'll know what to do," Max replied.

"Are you sure Max?" Tonkawa asked with hope in his voice.

"I can't explain it, Tonkawa, but he always knows what to do. Back home everyone goes to him whenever they need to solve a problem. If they need to fix something, they come to Grandpa. He always figures out just what to do."

Taru still felt confused. "He has experience with oil spills, does he?

Tonkawa just got kicked out of the clan for trusting you, and now you're asking us to trust another human being that we have never met? Not to mention, if we get caught by Koda trusting another human being, I will also be thrown out of the clan."

Max knew that asking Taru and Tonkawa to trust him was not a small request. Their very lives hung in the balance, but he also knew that they didn't know his grandfather.

"Listen," Max began, "you and Tonkawa can just wait in the woods, and if anything goes wrong you can just run away."

The two bears agreed as they hurried through the forest.

As they came running around the last bend before the cabin, Max said, "Ok, you wait here. I need to explain who you are before he meets you two. He's never going to believe this."

"I know how he feels," Taru replied, looking around and still feeling skeptical. Max ran up the steps and pushed open the cabin door.

Grandpa was standing at the desk beside the long range two-way radio. Next to the radio was Grandpa's pile of science magazines. He liked having all the classic science magazines and a few Max had never heard of.

Grandpa ran forward and pulled Max into a hug. "Max! Where have you been? I have been very worried about you! You were gone all night! I went down to the river and you were nowhere in sight. I was just getting ready to radio for help."

Max was breathing heavily. "I know Grandpa, and I am sorry. I got lost in exploring, but I have to tell you something! Something terrible has happened!"

"Take a deep breath and tell me what happened."

"You're not going to believe this, but I met a bear cub—a Spirit Bear just like you talked about! We played on the river, and he taught me how to fish, then his mother came and boy was she angry! She didn't want Tonkawa playing with me at all, but ..."

Just then Grandpa interrupted. "Okay, calm down, you're right, this one is a bit hard to swallow. You met a Spirit Bear cub and you were playing in the river?" Grandpa couldn't believe what Max was saying. "Are you sure you didn't fall asleep again and have one of your dreams?"

"No, no, Grandpa, I'm telling you the truth, but I have to tell you something else," Max said with urgency in his voice.

"Okay, slowly, tell me what happened," Grandpa said, trying to keep up.

"Okay," Max said as he took a deep breath, "I met this bear cub, and he's a white bear cub! You know, a Spirit Bear, and we became friends. We were playing on the river and his mother came out of the woods, and she is also a Spirit Bear. She's so beautiful, Grandpa! Anyway, she wasn't happy with Tonkawa, that's her cub's name, Tonkawa, and that he was playing with me, but Tonkawa explained to her how we met and how I stayed with him to keep him safe through the night. Then we all went walking through the woods. Grandpa, she knows so much about the woods and all the plants and animals that live here."

"Yes, I'm sure she would," Grandpa replied. Keeping his eyes fixed on Max, and beginning to worry his grandson might have fallen and hit his head, he slowly sat down in his chair.

"So, we were walking in the woods, then Tonkawa got kicked out of his bear clan, because he became friends with me!" Max was talking so fast he could hardly breathe.

Grandpa tried hard not to look with disbelief, as if Max was telling some tall tale. Grandpa knew that Max was an honest boy, but he also knew that he had a wild imagination. So he just listened as Max told his story.

"Then Tonkawa, Taru, and I walked up onto a high cliff that overlooks the waterways and rivers. We were sitting there when out of nowhere we saw this oil tanker coming down the inlet. It looked like it had lost power. As we were watching it, the bow rose up out of the water and the whole ship leaned to one side then slammed back down on the water, then suddenly it stopped! And then a black, brownish ooze came up from underneath the ship turning the water black, like ink, and it spread out further away from the ship!"

"Max, this is serious," Grandpa said sternly. "You're talking about an oil spill. You saw an oil tanker run aground and it's spilling oil out into the inlet?"

Max could tell that Grandpa was having a hard time believing him. He couldn't blame him, even Max thought the story sounded too fantastical as he told it, "Come, Grandpa, this will help you understand."

Max opened the cabin door and walked out onto the porch, "Grandpa come out here, I want you to meet my friends."

"Live in each season as it passes; breathe the air, drink the drink, taste the fruit, and resign yourself to the influence of the earth.

Henry David Thoreau

Chapter Ten

NOTHING COULD HAVE
PREPRARED THEM FOR THIS

Taru and Tonkawa and Grandpa stared at each other in disbelief for what seemed like an eternity.

"Max," Grandpa began, speaking slowly. As he did, Taru slowly put her paw in front of Tonkawa and moved him backward towards her. She began to growl and lowered her head.

"No, no, Taru, it's alright," Max said reassuringly.

"Max, we like you, but how do we know we can trust him?" Taru said holding Tonkawa back with her paw.

"What? Of course, you can. He's my grandfather. You can trust him because you trust me. You do trust me, right?" Max now understood why Taru was nervous. "You have nothing to worry about. My grandfather respects you and your home more than you could know. It's why we are here. It was my grandfather that wanted to teach me how to fish and teach me about the Great Bear Rainforest. He said this is the oldest rainforest of its kind on Earth and it needs to be protected.

Grandpa, seeing Taru still not convinced, began, "Taru, you and all the animals that live here mean the world to me and I can assure you I am a friend."

Taru replied, "You understand, Max's grandfather, that your kind hasn't given us many reasons to trust you."

"Yes, I do understand that," Grandpa began, "and I can't blame you for not trusting me, but I can assure you not all humans want to hurt you. There are many people who want to help you and I am one of them."

"Help?" Taru, asked with skepticism. "Well that's good, because we sure need some help right now."

"So, this oil tanker Max told me about — is it true?" Grandpa asked

"Yes, I'm afraid so," Taru replied.

"Can you take me to see it?" Grandpa asked.

Tonkawa jumped over Taru's protective paw and ran up beside Max. "We sure can! Come with us and we'll show you!"

Grandpa was caught by surprise at Tonkawa's fearlessness. "Well, my little friend, we best head to that cliff where you saw the tanker."

They ran through the forest, and in no time reached the cliff where they could look out over the waterway. There, lying on her side, was the oil tanker with oil spilling out. It looked as though the oil slick had spread further.

"Oh my," Grandpa gasped.

"Grandpa, what can we do?" Max asked.

Grandpa knew how Max looked up to him and thought that he had all the answers, but this time Grandpa was at a loss. He didn't know what to do. This was a big deal. He could see the hope in the eyes of Taru, Tonkawa, and Max. He didn't want to let them down.

Grandpa stood on the edge of the cliff thinking about the ecosystems that were now in serious danger. Feeling the despair of seeing such a catastrophe, he tried to think of what to do. He looked around them, and saw mushrooms growing from a rotting log. He stared at the mushrooms for what seemed like a very long time.

"Well," Taru said. "What are you thinking? Can you help us?"

Grandpa just kept staring at the mushroom.

Max stood beside him. "What is it Grandpa?"

Grandpa slowly turned his head to Max. Max knew that look. Max and Grandpa stood looking at each other. With just his eyes, Grandpa lead Max's eyes back to the ground where the mushrooms were growing.

"Max," Grandpa began in a low voice, in almost a whisper, "do you see what I am seeing?"

Max saw exactly what Grandpa was looking at. "Yes," Max replied.

"That's an Oyster mushroom."

"Okay …?" Max replied, not knowing why Grandpa was so fixated on this one particular mushroom. "What does that mean?"

"Well," Grandpa began, "last year, after I dropped you off at the bus station to go home, I was driving back to the farm and listening to that interview on the radio. I was interested because the guest was Paul Stamets, the mushroom scientist. You remember him right, Max?"

Max, still looking at the mushroom, replied, "Yes, of course I remember him."

"Well," Grandpa replied, "the radio host was interviewing Mr. Stamets about a mushroom he discovered that can dissolve oil. He was talking about oil remediation and stopping environmental damage from oil spills.

"What?" Max looked up into Grandpa's face. "A mushroom that eats oil?"

"Yes, Max, and I am sure this is it." Grandpa was recalling the interview from over a year ago. "Mr. Stamets explained how he injects these Oyster mushrooms into straw booms. He called them Mycobooms."

"Okay," Max said. "How do these Mycobooms work?"

"Well, apparently these straw booms are injected with this Oyster mushroom and they become Mycobooms. Then they are placed in and around the oil spill, and depending on the oil load, once the mycelium exudes enzymes, they break down these long chain complex hydrocarbons and a domino effect begins. The sunlight, because of the UV rays, along with bacteria, start breaking down the oil into a simple sugar, and then the oil dissolves."

Taru tilted her head sideways, confused, and asked, "Max, what is he talking about? What's a hypercoupon?"

"No, no!" Max began to laugh. "He said hydrocarbons. Grandpa is saying that there are mushrooms that break down oil."

"Okay, now I've heard everything." Taru sat down hard, feeling confused. Grandpa looked at Taru and said, "I know exactly how you feel, but if you

knew Paul Stamets, you'd understand."

Max, turning to Grandpa, asked, "What do we do?"

"I think I still have Mr. Stamets' phone number. Let's go back to the cabin and use the satellite phone and try to call him." Grandpa was feeling hopeful.

Tonkawa had been sitting quietly listening. "Max, can your grandfather help us? Does he know what to do?"

"Tonkawa, like I said, whenever there is a problem, he figures out what to do," Max replied.

"Hang on boys," Grandpa interrupted. "I don't always figure out what to do, but one thing I do know — there is always someone who does know the answer. And more often than not, as Paul Stamets says, the answers are right under our feet."

Taru looked up with a smile. "So what you're saying is, you do know what to do?" And they all started laughing.

Looking at the oil spill disaster in the river, "Let's get back to the cabin." Grandpa said with an urgent calmness in his voice. "We need to make that call, and quickly,"

"In every walk with nature one receives far more than he seeks.

John Muir

Chapter Eleven

IF YOU LISTEN VERY CAREFULLY

Walking through the old growth forest, Paul Stamets listened to the sounds of nature. Communicating with nature required listening and observing.

"Nature speaks to us in her silence, and sometimes she is not so silent," he would say. It was something Paul had learned over his forty years of exploring and studying ecosystems of the forests.

Paul called Agarikon Island home, located off the coast of British Columbia, Canada. It was here that Paul established his global reputation as the world's leading mycologist. Paul had spent years in the old growth forests of Washington State, but it was here on Agarikon Island that Paul came to immerse himself in the solitude of nature. It was here that he listened to what nature was trying to tell all of us.

Paul was known for inventing ways to replace toxic pesticides with natural mushroom-based "mycopesticides." He developed water filtration systems called "mycofiltration." This was a method to clean water using mycelium. He also developed a way to clean up oil spills. It was for this reason that Grandpa felt the urgency to call Mr. Stamets.

Paul walked across an ancient fallen Red Cedar tree with familiarity and balance, as if he was walking down a sidewalk. Then his phone began to ring.

"Hello, this is Paul. Who am I speaking with?"

"Hello, Mr. Stamets? I'm calling you with an urgent issue. Do you have time to speak?"

"Well, why don't you start by telling me who you are," Paul asked cautiously.

"Oh yes, of course. Last year my grandson, Max, and I called you from Ohio regarding the honey bee and Colony Collapse Disorder. You were very gracious and helpful. You sent us gallons of liquid mycelium extract to mix with the bees' drinking water," Grandpa explained.

"Oh yes, hello! How are you my friend, and how is that brilliant grandson of yours?"

"He is doing great, Mr. Stamets, but I have to say we have a serious challenge. You see, Max and I are up here in the Great Bear Rainforest on Gribbell Island, and there has been a disaster. An oil tanker has run aground and is spilling oil into the waterway!" Grandpa said with a disheartened urgency.

"It was only a matter of time, I'm afraid," Paul replied. "You want to know if my mycoremediation method will work, is that right?"

"Well, yes, exactly. Is there any way you could come out here and see the disaster for yourself?" Grandpa asked hopefully.

"I actually need to in order to assess what it will required to contain that spill. But, tell me, is the tide coming in or going out?" Paul didn't let on how concerned he was because he didn't want to alarm him. Paul understood more than anyone the dangerous situation that was unfolding and how it could affect the ecosystems of the rivers, channels, and waterways of the Great Bear Rainforest.

"I believe it is going out, Mr. Stamets. Is that important?" Grandpa asked.

"If the tide is going out then we have time to protect the immediate ecosystems, but if that tide should turn, well—just call me right away when the tide turns."

"Yes, of course. Is there anything else we can do while we wait for you, Mr. Stamets?" Grandpa asked.

"One last thing," Paul said. "Call me Pablo—my friends call me Pablo."

Smiling, Grandpa replied, "Okay, Pablo." Grandpa disconnected the call feeling a little more reassured.

" . . . and then, I have nature and art and poetry, and if that is not enough, what is enough?

Vincent van Gogh

Chapter Twelve

AT LEAST I'M TRYING.
HOW MANY PEOPLE ARE NOT TRYING?

Paul immediately called the Erickson Aircrane company in Portland, Oregon.

"Erickson Aircrane company, Andy speaking. How can I help you?"

"Andy, it's Paul Stamets, have you got a minute? It's urgent!"

"Hello Mr. Stamets, of course. What's going on?"

"Well, there's been an oil spill up near the Great Bear Rainforest, near Gribbell Island. I was wondering if you had an air-crane nearby up there?"

"That is urgent. Hang on, Mr. Stamets, let me check the assignment logs."

After checking the assignment logs, Andy returned to the phone. "Good news! Not only do we have one up there, but your daughter, Captain Ladena, is there now too."

"Looks like this is our lucky day, Andy," Pablo said with relief.

"Yes, it is! The crane was leased to the Canadian government to help with some forest fires they were having trouble with. They also wanted our best pilot, so we sent Ladena up there."

"Fantastic!" Pablo said. "Tell her I'm headed up there now to assess an oil spill. Ask her if she will be available to work with us."

"Of course. Knowing her, she'll insist on it."

"I need to get there immediately to assess the situation. After I make my assessment, I'll need you to get that helicopter to Hartley Bay Airport."

"Well, hang on, now. You know the payload limit is 20,000 pounds?"

Pablo smiled. "Not to worry, Andy, my guess is that will be enough."

"Okay! Just call when you're ready. In the meantime, I'll give our LeDena a heads up."

"Thank you so much! Talk to you soon."

"Hang on, Mr. Stamets, where are you now?"

"I'm here at my home on Agarikon Island."

"How are you getting to Gribbell Island?"

"I haven't worked that part out yet."

"Listen, I'm sending you our de Havilland Canada DHC-3 Otter sea plane. It's perfect. Short takeoff and landing, about 1000-mile range. It's also a high-wing, so you'll be able to assess a lot of the spill from the air with no wing obstruction. Be out on your deck in about an hour."

"Thank you, my friend. Let's hope that tide doesn't change before we can secure this site."

Packing his duffle bag, Pablo thought about all the details and people he needed to contact, not to mention the many steps he needed to choreograph with perfect timing in order to pull this off. Fortunately, Pablo thought to himself, using these new Mycobooms, the remote location of this spill isn't going to be a problem for us, but that tide certainly could be. For that reason alone, I need to make sure this is timed perfectly.

Standing down on his dock, Pablo waited for the sea plane and made another call.

"David, Pablo here." David was in charge of the Mycoboom production at the Stamets Mycoremediation Center in Olympia, Washington. Pablo needed to find out how many Mycobooms were in inventory.

"Hello, Pablo, what's going on?"

"I need your help. We have a crisis on our hands and it could turn into a disaster unless we can act quickly."

"Ok, sure, tell me what happened."

Pablo explained the situation to David. "And I have a plan, Mycobooms. How many do we have available?"

"Fortunately, we just finished this month's production. We have about sixty Mycobooms ready to go and another fifty almost ready. The mycelium has taken hold."

"That's great! I need all of them, but we'll still need more. This may not be the largest spill we have faced, but it could cause the most harm to wildlife and ecosystems because of its location."

"How are we going to get that done?"

"It will be challenging, but it's doable. We have to try. We each have a responsibility to take help take care of this planet in whatever way we can. How many people are not trying?" David paused for a moment and thought about Pablo's question.

"Listen carefully," Pablo began. "Go down to Valley Dairy Farm – they have just finished haying their fields and have hundreds of bales. Ask for Prescott, he owns the farm. Tell him what happened, and that we only need twenty-five bales. Make sure to tell him you work with me."

"Will twenty-five bales be enough Pablo?" David asked.

"Each bale of hay weighs a thousand pounds, so that gives us about ten Mycobooms per bale. Twenty-five bales will give us an additional two-hundred and fifty Mycobooms. That will give us three-hundred and sixty booms total, and that will be enough to cover over a mile-long spill."

"Great idea, but we need to create the booms and inject with mycelium."

"Get everybody to come to the farm and have them call their friends. Let's aim for about ten people per bail and give each person one Mycoboom sleeve bag to stuff. It's only a hundred pounds, so that should be easy enough. As they finish, you are in charge of the injecting process—you know what to do, and it won't take you long. Once you are finished call me."

"I'm on it."

"And, David?"

"Yeah?"

"Not only are the ecosystems of the Great Bear Rainforest at risk here, as if that isn't bad enough, but the Spirit Bear is as well. Let everybody know, okay?"

"You got it, Pablo. I'll call you when we are done."

"Nature always wears the colors of the spirit.

Ralph Waldo Emerson

Chapter Thirteen

ANSWERING THE CALL

As Pablo hung up the phone, he could hear the roar of the Otter Sea Plane's engine humming.

Pablo watched as the plane dropped into a steep dive over Agarikon Island onto Desolation Sound, Pablo's home. The Otter was famous for its short and steep landing and take-off capabilities. It looked as though it was going to dive straight into the water, when, at the last minute, the pilot eased back on the throttle and leveled off the plane. As it touched down, its water pontoons skipped across the water. The engine calmed down to an idle and the pilot brought the plane up to Pablo's dock.

"There's only one crazy person I know who can fly like that!" Pablo yelled, trying to speak over the idling engine.

The door popped open.

"Jimmy! I knew that was you! Only you could drop in like that."

"Pablo, so good to see you!" As Jimmy stepped onto the dock, he gave Pablo a big hug. "So good to see you, brother. I heard about the situation up near Gribbell Island. Andy told me—it doesn't sound good."

"No, not at all," Pablo replied.

"What are you planning?" Jimmy asked.

"Let's get going, I'll tell you all about it on the way." Pablo handed Jimmy his duffle bag and climbed into the plane.

Jimmy loaded Pablo's duffle bag in the storage compartment and climbed into the cockpit. "Buckle in, Pablo." Jimmy motioned to Pablo, and then started the engine. It roared to life. Pushing the throttle forward, Jimmy pulled away from the dock and taxied out into Desolation Sound. "Here we go! I'll have you there before you know it."

"The nitrogen in our DNA, the calcium in our teeth, the iron in our blood, the carbon in our apple pies was made in the interiors of collapsing stars. We are made of star stuff.

Carl Sagan

Chapter Fourteen

IT TAKES A TEAM

"Great job everyone, we just created 360 Mycobooms—36,000 pounds of oil-eating Oyster Mycobooms!" David said, congratulating his team of volunteers. As David stood there, he began to wonder how he was going to transport all the Mycobooms to the Great Bear Rainforest. Just then his phone rang.

"David, it's Pablo, how are we doing?"

"Great, Pablo! The booms are made and injected with the Oyster mushroom mycelium. We have 360 Mycobooms and we're ready to go. What do you…"Just as David started to get the words out, two flatbed semi-trucks came rolling into the farm.

"You should be seeing two flatbed trucks coming into the farm now," Pablo said.

David stood there and just smiled. "I should have known you would have this planned."

"One last request, David, if you don't mind," Pablo said.

"No problem, Pablo," David replied.

"Help those truck drivers load those booms? They are on a tight schedule. They need to get to the Port of Vancouver right away."

"Not to worry! We will help them!" David said reassuringly.

"Thank you! I appreciate all your help. Tell everybody I said thank you. You may just helped save an entire ecosystem," Pablo said with gratitude and hung up his phone.

David gave instructions to the team. "Okay everyone let's get these loaded! Timing is everything!"

It took a few hours to load the trucks, but finally they were ready to go. The truck drivers had their instructions to get the Mycobooms to the Port of Vancouver, a four-hour drive.

As their trucks pulled away to make their journey up to Vancouver, the team stood together, cheering the truck drivers on!

Back in the plane, Jimmy had overheard all of Pablo's conversation. "So, what you are planning on doing up in the Great Bear Rainforest?"

"Jimmy, I have to tell you—I'm worried. An oil tanker was coming down the inlet and it lost power. Drifting, it ran aground on rocks. It's spilling thousands of gallons per minute as we speak."

"Why are they allowing tankers the use of those waterways? We all know how fragile those ecosystems are up there. What's going on?"

"It's really quite remarkable. The Great Bear Rainforest began its battle in the 1990's. Today about one-third of the Great Bear Rainforest is protected, but the animals are not, if you can believe that, and now a new threat is coming.

"The Trans Mountain tar sands oil pipeline will ship nearly a million barrels of the dirtiest oil in the world to the coast. They will use the waterways to navigate the tankers down to the sea. Tankers again navigate the narrow, rocky channels to make their way to Hecate Strait, a major shipping artery. It is from there, they make their way up to Prince Rupert and then they head out to the Gulf of Alaska, and then on to China. One spill along any of the waterways could threaten entire ecosystems. This spill has the potential of being that spill." As Pablo explained this, he looked out the window down to the waterways below. He could see a large pod of orcas. There had to be at least forty orcas making their way up the coast.

"Look at that, Jimmy! A large pod of orcas!"

"What a sight, huh?" said Jimmy, looking below. "They are so fascinating. I have become very concerned for these animals. I see them occasionally while flying over these coastal routes."

"I worry about the transient pods," Pablo replied. "They feed almost exclusively on marine animals. Offshore orcas feed on schooling fish and sharks since they are far out in the Pacific Ocean. The resident northern and southern orcas feed on coastal fish, primarily salmon and squid. If just one oil spill disaster should happen, that would not endanger the food supply, but also the orcas directly, and that has me very concerned."

"Look deep into nature, and then you will understand everything better.

Albert Einstein

Chapter Fifteen

KNOWING ISN'T ENOUGH

Pablo looked out the window to the orcas below and started to think about the ocean's food chain and how the ecosystems are all interconnected.

"These oil spills are a dangerous threat to these magnificent mammals," Jimmy acknowledged.

"I'm afraid it's more complicated than that," Pablo began. "Ship interactions have increased due to more commercialization, and that means that the acoustics needed for echolocation are affected. Orca communication suffers the consequences. Additionally, more fisheries contribute to increased accidental net entrapments and this also contributes to decreased prey availability. See, this is what I am talking about when I talk about the delicate interconnectedness of ecosystems."

"Certainly with all we know, can't something can be done?" Jimmy asked.

"Jimmy, knowledge alone doesn't guarantee change or even survival. Knowledge must have the spirit of the heart come into it, which causes clear understanding. That is how a paradigm shift happens," Pablo replied.

"It seems, Pablo," Jimmy offered, "that the people who do not care or have any regard for the balance of nature move into powerful decision-making positions, yet they are blinded by some other agenda."

"What I have learned is this: careless people can alter positive change. Just as we move closer to understanding, corruption surfaces to withstand the change."

"When you put it like that, I feel there isn't much we can do," Jimmy replied.

"There are many truths, Jimmy. I believe nature is a force for good. Good is not only a concept, it is a spirit, and so hopefully the spirit of goodness will survive."

"So which truth wins?" Jimmy asked.

"The one we feed, Jimmy. The one we feed," Pablo replied, looking at his watch.

Jimmy looked below to the dark mass of orcas, moving as one living organism floating up the coast, and thought deeply about Pablo's words.

" If you knew that every breath you took could save hundreds of lives in the future, had you walked down this path of knowledge, wouldn't you run down that path of knowledge as fast as you could?

Paul Stamets

Chapter Sixteen

SOMETIMES THE ANSWERS
ARE RIGHT UNDER OUR FEET

Taru, Tonkawa, and Max sat watching the oil spill closely, watching for any sign of the tide changing. Fortunately, the tide turns in and out every six hours and low low tide every 24 hours. The tide had not turned.

"Why did Mr. Stamets want us to watch the tide so closely?" Tonkawa asked.

"Well, Tonkawa, I imagine it has something to do with that oil moving up the inlet and affecting all those ecosystems along the way. As long as the tide is moving out, the inner coastal ecosystems are safe."

"Safe?" Tonkawa asked.

"We don't need to worry about that now, Tonkawa," Grandpa replied reassuringly. "The tide is still going out."

By now, all the creatures of the forest had heard that Taru and Tonkawa were sitting up on the cliff with humans! One by one, a wolf, a wolverine, and a deer walked out of the forest and stood by Taru. Even Owl came silently gliding in and perched on the branch above Taru's head.

"Hello there," Taru greeted the other animals. "Nice to see you all! Tell me," she said, looking out at the tanker ship, "don't you see the humans here?" She smiled to herself.

The wolverine, who had no patience for anyone, replied, "Yeah, we see 'em."

"Aren't you afraid?"

"The way we figure it, Taru, the fact they're sitting this close to your cub, you've either lost your mind or you guys are up to something. Either way, we wanted to find out what is going on."

Taru pointed to the tanker. "Well, look out there—there's an oil spill."

The animals began to panic. "Oh no! What happened?"

"Now hang on," Grandpa said calmly, and at once all the animals stopped and stared at Grandpa, stunned to hear him speak. The animals had never heard a human before. Taru shot Grandpa a look and Grandpa knew exactly what she meant.

"With respect to you all," Grandpa continued, "my grandson and I mean you no harm. We are here to help you. As you can see, there is a serious situation on the river." They all looked out to the tanker leaning to one side with oil seeping into the river. "I do not want you to worry. We called someone, and he is coming to help."

"More humans?" the wolverine asked with concern.

"Yes," Grandpa replied.

The wolverine looked at Taru. "Taru, you know what humans are capable of, and you know how unpredictable they are. Do I need to point out the obvious?" He motioned to the oil tanker out on the river.

"Yes, Wolverine, I am well aware, but you need to understand as Tonkawa and I have come to understand, not all humans are bad. Actually, there are many who want to understand us better and they want to help us. Such a man is on his way."

"Great, another human." Wolverine rolled his eyes. "Well, I know a certain bear that will be furious when he finds out, and so do you, Taru." Wolverine was referring to Koda.

"Well, for one thing," Max interrupted, "it's because of this man the bees were saved from extinction."

With wide eyes of surprise, Wolverine replied, "He did what?"

"He helped save bees from extinction, and knowing him, he is going to make that oil spill disappear," Max replied.

"Okay, now I've heard everything. Taru, now we know you've lost your mind. Let's go everyone, we've heard enough," Wolverine said sarcastically.

"No, Wolverine, he's telling you the truth," Taru replied.

"And how is he going to make oil disappear? Look at that mess."

Grandpa stood up and walked over to the log to where he first noticed the Oyster mushrooms. Grandpa held out his hand to show Wolverine and the other animals the mushroom. "He's going to do it with this."

"And you're telling us that this tiny mushroom is going to get rid of all that?" Wolverine said, pointing his nose towards the oil spill.

"Actually, yes, but it's not quite that simple. Let me explain," Grandpa replied.

"Just a minute," Wolverine interrupted, sitting down on the soft moss. "Let

me get comfortable. I can't wait to hear this."

The animals gathered around as Grandpa began to explain the process that Paul Stamets invented to clean up oil spills.

"You see, this mushroom has a unique characteristic. It has the ability to absorb oil and break it down into simple sugars, and then the oil dissolves."

Wolverine still couldn't believe what he was hearing. "So, you're telling us that if you throw a bunch of those mushrooms into that mess, the oil will dissolve?"

"Well, yes, actually," Grandpa replied. "You see, they fill these long burlap cloth tubes with straw. This creates booms that are about twenty feet long. They then inject the boom with the mycelium, the root system of the Oyster mushroom." Grandpa bent down and lifted up a piece of the rotting bark where the mushrooms were growing. "You see this white, web-like stuff here?" He pointed to the root system of the mushroom. "This is called mycelium, and Paul Stamets discovered that if he takes a small piece of this and places it in the straw boom, within a few weeks the mycelium uses the straw as a food source and will convert most of the straw into mycelium."

"Okay, we're with you so far," Wolverine said looking amazed, as did all the animals. Even Taru and Tonkawa were amazed, because this was the first time they were hearing exactly how this was going to work.

"You then take these Mycobooms," Grandpa continued, "and place them around the oil to corral the oil. You then place additional Mycobooms inside the perimeter of the contained oil, and let the mushrooms go to work."

"You've got to be kidding, right? We had no idea!" Wolverine exclaimed.

"Nobody did until Paul Stamets discovered it." Max replied.

"So, Paul Stamets is coming here?" Wolverine asked.

"Yes, he is," Grandpa replied. "To try and help you all."

Wolverine looked at Taru. "No wonder you like these guys, Taru," he said, smiling. "I think I like them too!" All the animals nodded their heads in agreement.

"It's never too late to be what you might have been.

George Eliot

Chapter Seventeen

IT'S FURTHER THAN YOU THINK

The semi-trucks pulled into the Port of Vancouver, driving down to the docks and right up to the Fungi Perfecti Mycotransport sea plane waiting by the dock.

The Fungi Perfecti Mycotransport sea plane was actually a repurposed Albatross. It was used by the U.S. Air Force, primarily in the search and rescue mission role (SAR), where it gained a reputation as a rugged and seaworthy plane. It was essentially a flying boat. This plane requires two people to operate it, a pilot and a copilot, and teamwork. The Albatross was so efficient as a search and rescue craft that the Air National Guard, U.S. Coast Guard, U.S. Navy and the Royal Canadian Air Force operated the Albatross as a coastal and long-range open ocean search and rescue aircraft.

In 2010, Paul Stamets purchased one and had it converted to what is called Standard Category. This meant that the Albatross could be used in private operation. The plane went through extensive modifications. Engineers installed new twin engines, stainless steel engine oil tanks, and state-of-the-art navigation systems, as well as made modifications to the doors to accommodate the twenty-foot Mycobooms. Upon completion, it was renamed Fungi Perfecti Mycotransport (FPM). This now meant that Fungi Perfecti had the capability to deliver Mycobooms to remote areas of coastal and the open ocean, as well as remote dry land spill sites.

Two brothers, Captains Owen and Reid Marshall, were hired as full-time pilots for the Fungi Perfecti Mycotransport plane. They became full time pilots because oil spills happen more often than people realize, but cannot be predicted. The pilots are on call 24 hours a day, 7 days a week, 365 days a year.

Captains Owen and Reid Marshall came up the dock to greet the drivers. "Hello there," Captain Owen said, introducing himself and his brother. "We

are the captains of the Fungi Perfecti Mycotransport plane (FPM). Let's get these loaded! We are on a tight schedule."

It took two hours to load all the Mycobooms. At only a hundred pounds each, they loaded easily. The Mycobooms had more than enough room on the FPM. This plane had a max load weight capacity of 37,000 pounds, with an overall length of sixty feet and a height of twenty-five feet, so there was no problem loading all 360 Mycobooms. Mycobooms are twenty feet in length; that's over one mile of oil-eating Oyster mushroom power..

"Let's go, Owen," Reid called to his brother. He turned to the truck drivers. "Thanks guys, for all your help."

"Happy to help! Good luck!" the truck drivers called back.

The twin engines of the FPM kicked in and came to life as the propellers began to rotate on command. "We'd better radio Pablo and let him know we're on our way," Captain Owen suggested.

"Good idea. Let's see if we can reach him." Captain Reid put on his communication head set, "Pablo, this is the FPM, come in. Over..." He waited a moment and then repeated, "Pablo, this is the FPM, come in. Over..."

Pablo's voice came crackling into Captain Reid'sheadset. Pablo replied, "Hello FPM, Pablo here. Are you on your way? Over..."

"Yes, indeed Pablo, we are in the air and loaded with Mycobooms. Over..."
"Great news! When do you think you expect to arrive? Over..."

"If we push it, our ETA should be just under three hours. Over..."

"Great, we really need you guys. Fly safely. Over and out."

Captain Reid turned to his brother. "Well, you heard him, Owen, they need these Mycobooms. Let's kick this into gear."

With that, Captain Reid pushed the throttle forward and the FPM accelerated to 225 miles per hour.

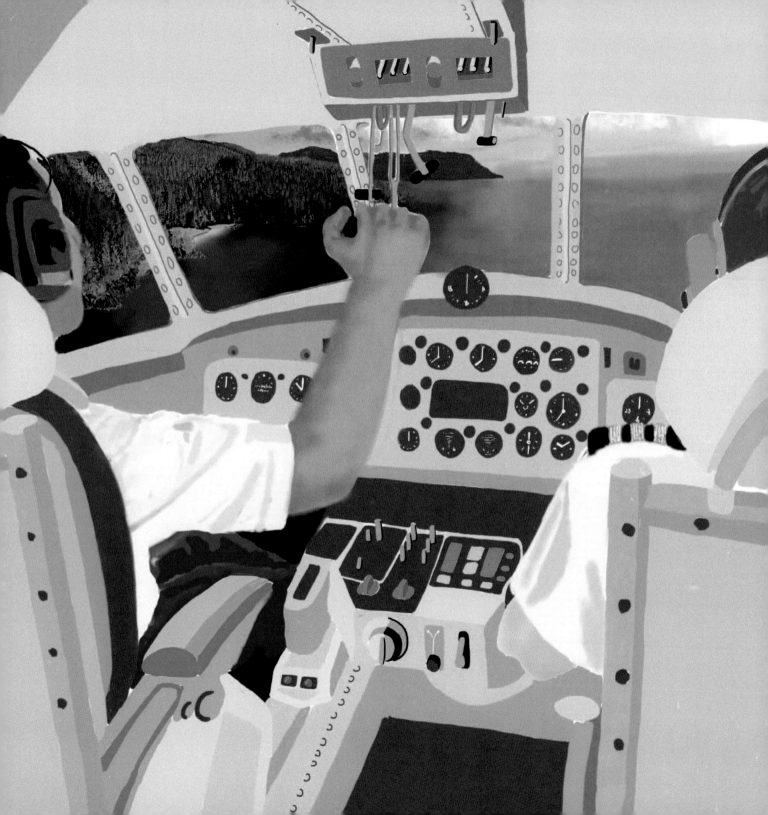

"Science and technology revolutionize our lives, but memory, tradition, [story] and myth frame our response.

Arthur M. Schlesinger

Chapter Eighteen

MAYDAY! MAYDAY!

As Jimmy was checking his navigation systems, he asked, "Pablo, have you ever seen a Spirit Bear?"

"No, Jimmy, I have not. Tell me, with all the years you have been flying this territory, have you?"

"Actually, I have. I was flying up to Hartley Bay, over the lakes of Gribbell Island. The hidden lakes there are truly beautiful, like none I have ever seen. I approached from the east side entrance to Douglas Channel at Wright Sound. It was raining and there was some fog. As I came in low I noticed a group of mostly black bears with two white bears fishing in one of the lakes. As I approached, all the black bears disappeared back into the forest, but the white bears didn't move. They just looked up at me and continued fishing. I always wondered why that was."

"Well, Jimmy, there is a theory. The Spirit Bear is much more docile and calm than their black bear sisters and brothers. Nobody really understands why. They also have a better fishing success rate."

"Why is that?" Jimmy asked with surprise.

"Think like a fish for minute, Jimmy. When you're under the water and a dark mass moves over you, not only are you alarmed, but your instinct tells you that there is danger approaching. When a white mass moves over you, you're not startled because it's something you see every day, it's just a cloud. It's believed this is one of the reasons for the Spirit Bear's survival–they eat more often and can maintain a healthy life cycle."

"Then why are there so few of them?" Jimmy asked.

"That has to do with the genetic lottery. For every ten black bears born there might be only one white bear born. It's rare to see them, and it's even more rare to see a Spirit Bear cub." Pablo sighed. "I don't know, Jimmy. If we don't succeed in cleaning up this oil spill, these bears could be in danger of extinction."

Just as Pablo finished his sentence, the engines chocked and stalled, then started, then chocked and stalled.

"What is it, Jimmy? Are we having trouble?"

"Not sure, she's never done this before. I think I might have water in the fuel line. I better take her down."

Fortunately, emergency landing with a sea plane was very easy. All Jimmy had to do was pick a calm area of water and take her down. "Hang on, Pablo! I'm going to land her down there on Kitlope Lake. It's our best option."

Jimmy pushed the throttle forward and navigated the plane to a shallow descent. Pulling back slightly on the throttle stick, the pontoons skipped across the water then settled into a full landing.

As Jimmy steered the boat to the shore, Pablo asked, "What do you think Jimmy?"

"I need to check things out." Jimmy opened his door and climbed out of his seat. Stepping into the water, he pushed the plane up onto the beach as far as he could. He lifted the engine cover, and began to examine the engine, looking for the trouble.

While Jimmy worked, Pablo walked along the shore studying the plants and the growth thickly crowding the shore line.

Wiping his hands on his oil rag, Jimmy said, "No wonder we had smoke. Looks like we have a hole in the oil filter. We are stuck."

"Well," Pablo began, "let's get on the radio and see if we can get some help."

"Okay," Jimmy replied, feeling less than hopeful. "But even if we reach someone, it will be days before they get to us. Unfortunately, this is one of the most remote areas we could have landed."

"What do you suggest we do?" Pablo asked. "We can't just sit here, of all times not now."

Jimmy tried using the radio, but he was getting no signal. He walked over to the little utility door on side of his plane and pulled out a flare gun. "We could always try this."

"Ever use that before?" Pablo asked.

"No, can't say I have. Never needed to," Jimmy replied as he took his flare gun and fired. The flare shot high into the air and burst; it hung in the air, then arched downward, burning out as it fell.

"Let's see what happens," Jimmy said.

"Well, I'm hungry, how about you?" Pablo said.

"No problem Pablo, I think I have some rations in the food locker in the plane."
"That's great."

After checking the food locker, "Well, bad news, Pablo, I didn't fill the food locker before I took off, so there isn't much." Jimmy held out his hand with a few candy bars and a bag of peanuts. "Sorry, Pablo."

"No worries, Jimmy. There is a buffet at our feet. Start a fire, and I'll be right back." Pablo walked into the forest and was gone for no more than ten minutes before he came back with an armful of various kinds of mushrooms and herbs.

"Here we are! Did you get that fire going yet?"

"Wait; what? My gosh, Pablo, you just left. Hang on, and I'll get this fire going," Jimmy replied as he gathered more sticks and twigs.

Pablo walked down to the water to wash the mushrooms, leaves, and herbs he had picked, steamed the Broadleaf Plantain leaves, and then rolled up all his mushrooms and herbs inside the leaves. "These Plantain leaves aren't the tastiest of the wild plants to consume Jimmy, but they are well known for their nutritional and medicinal benefits," Pablo explained as he placed them on the fire and sat down next to Jimmy.

"You're going to love this," Pablo said, smiling.

"What exactly did you put in there?" Jimmy asked curiously.

"There is a whole host of food laying at our feet—we need to know what to look for. I found some mushrooms, sprouts, berries, roots, and rhizomes, and I even gathered some seaweed."

"Pablo, you'd make a great wilderness pilot!"

"Traditionally," Pablo began, "root vegetables were held in high regard by First Nations. Root vegetables were an important food source and used for ceremonial reasons. Some nations held First Roots ceremonies to show respect for the roots before the community went digging for their food. They even used them for economic reasons, trading them and storing them as a back-up food supply in times of shortage."

"When did you know learn what to pick?" Jimmy asked.

"When you spend as much time as I do out deep in the old growth forests, you learn a thing or two, Jimmy. Like my brother used to say, 'It's not enough to grow old, you have to pay attention.'" They both laughed.

Taking the leaves off the fire, Pablo unwrapped them. Inside was a beautiful mixture of roasted mushrooms, berries, herbs, roots, and rhizomes.

Jimmy took a scoop with his fingers and popped them into his mouth. "This is delicious, Pablo!"

"Thank you, Jimmy. There is so much the Earth gives us if we could only learn to see while we're looking," Pablo replied.

"Hello, there!" a voice called from a riverboat pulling up to the shore. "I assume that flare was from you guys?"

"Hello!" Jimmy and Pablo said at the same time. Caught up in conversation, they hadn't heard the boat approach.

"Yes, that would be us. Thank you for coming!" Jimmy said, so happy to see him. "My name is Jimmy, and this is Pablo."

"Glad to meet you both! My name is Trevon. I am the lead guide for Wilderness Expeditions. I was cruising the waterways and I saw your flare. Good thing too, because there isn't another soul for miles. What is the problem?" Trevon asked.

"Looks like I have a hole in my oil filter and..." Jimmy began to reply, but Trevon interrupted.

"Don't tell me—you don't have a spare on hand?"

"Unfortunately, no," Jimmy said.

"I'm afraid I won't be able to reach anyone by radio, but I can take you up to Hartley Bay. It's only about an hour boat ride. They have an airport there.

"Hartley Bay Airport, yes, of course," Pablo said with relief. "That is where we are headed."

"There's an oil spill up there," Trevon said. "A tanker lost power and ran up on some rocks. It's a real mess."

"Yes, that's why I am going there," Pablo replied.

Trevon knew everything that went on around the rivers and waterways. He had grown up helping his father, who spent his life as a river guide. It didn't take Trevon long to learn all his father knew about the rivers, the fjords, and the lakes, and now he had earned a legendary reputation as a river guide. Conservationists, naturalists, and many scientists would have to book Trevon two years in advance to take them through the dizzying maze of rivers and fjords. "I'll take Pablo up to the airport, and send the rescue boat back for you, Jimmy. They will have all you need to get your bird flying again."

"That would be great, Trevon. Thank you," Jimmy said.

Pablo said goodbye to Jimmy and climbed into the boat with Trevon.

"Wait, Pablo, what about all this food?" Jimmy asked, overwhelmed.

"You eat it Jimmy — it will be one of the best meals you'll ever have." Pablo said, waving.

Reassuring Jimmy they would send someone back to help, Trevon pulled the chord on his engine and they headed to Hartley Bay Airport.

"Science is not only compatible with spirituality; it is a profound source of spirituality.

Carl Sagan

Chapter Nineteen

IT'S ALL SO FASCINATING

As they sped up the river, Trevon asked, "So you're here to help with the oil spill?"

"I developed a process using mushrooms that can dissolve oil," Pablo explained, "so, I am here because I think I can help."

"What process have you developed where mushrooms can clean up oil?" Trevon asked feeling skeptical.

"To explain that, I first need to tell you that in the early 1990's, I developed a way to capture beneficial nutrients that mushrooms offer inherently and use them to support innate immunity in us. Mushrooms and humans, it turns out, have quite a few things in common.

"We share more of our DNA with mushrooms than with any other Kingdom. Mushrooms can naturally extend to humans the art of immunity they've perfected over millions of years. In the wild they contend against the same pathogens that afflict us; their native defense we can use to our own advantage."

"Wait," Trevon interrupted. "You mean we share that much of our DNA with mushrooms?"

"Yes, and that's not all," Paul continued. "The root system of mushrooms, called mycelium, is only one cell wall thick. So, as I mentioned, they are extremely good at protecting themselves from the pathogens they face in the wild. Many of these pathogens happen to be the same pathogens that afflict us. Mushrooms are extremely beneficial for us."

Trevon couldn't believe what he was hearing. Fascinated by what Pablo was teaching him, he listened very carefully.

"Beyond supporting human immunity," Paul continued, "mushrooms and mycelium, the root-like structure where the mushroom organism spends most of its life, are decomposers of the natural world. They transform what's old and dead into new life, regenerating soil and ecosystems. Without mycelium there would be no soil."

"Slow down. I am trying to comprehend everything you're saying. How did you ever even begin to know to look at mushrooms?" Trevon asked, fascinated.

"The Earth has gone through several major extinctions, and mushrooms survived while many other organisms like large animals did not. Don't you find that fascinating? I do—and I had to know why. If you knew that every breath you took could save hundreds of lives in the future, had you walked down this path of knowledge, wouldn't you run down that path as fast as you could?"

"Yes, but what you're talking about is saving the planet, and isn't that just too big of a challenge?" Trevon asked.

"I love a challenge, Trevon, and saving people and planet is probably a good one!"

As Pablo and Trevon traveled up the river, they sat in silence. Looking up at the Douglas fir growing close to the river, soaring as high as 250 feet, Pablo thought about the life the trees sustained. Not just the hundreds of ecosystems that flourished there, but how the trees were widely used among coastal First Nations. The Western Red Cedar was an evergreen that grew slowly—some were more than a thousand years old. Known by indigenous people as the "Tree of Life," the tree was perfect for totem carving because the wood naturally repelled fungus and insects and didn't easily warp or twist. The wood was also easier to paint and stain, because the tree didn't contain any resin or pitch. The Red Cedars fiber was used to make clothing. The wood, both rot-resistant and water resistant, was used for buildings and structures, furniture making, canoes, and guitars. The oil of the trees was perfect for skin treatments and perfumes. Human life evolved in places similar to this. But if we continued the way we were headed, we would destroy them, and we would destroy ourselves.

This one place, The Great Bear Rainforest, was home to some of the oldest and largest trees on Earth. You won't find a more pristine region on Earth than the North Coast and Central Coast of B.C Canada.

" We can judge our progress by the courage of our questions and the depth of our answers, our willingness to embrace what is true rather than what feels good.

Carl Sagan

Chapter Twenty

HELP HAS ARRIVED

"Do you see any sign of him?" Tonkawa asked, looking out over the cliff anxiously for Pablo to arrive.

Max, Grandpa, Tonkawa, Taru, and all the animals sat on the cliff watching the tanker leak more oil into the waterway. Everyone was nervous, hoping they would see Pablo's plane come flying over the mountains any minute.

"He'll be here shortly," Grandpa replied calmly. "I am sure he is doing everything he can to get here as quickly as he can. Keep in mind, he doesn't work alone, and these efforts take a lot of coordination."

Just then, as Grandpa was explaining some of what Pablo had to coordinate, Koda came bursting through the trees. "There you are Taru! I thought I was very clear about Tonkawa, and now I find you with that human boy and now I see yet another HUMAN! He is what killed Hotah!"

"No, Koda!" Taru yelled back. "Thoughtless, careless men killed Hotah, not Max and his grandfather! They are trying to help us!"

Full of rage, Koda began to charge Taru, but as he began charging, all the animals formed a line in front of Tonkawa, Taru, Max, and Grandpa. At the same time, Owl flew down from his branch and hovered in front of Koda's face.

"You will go no further, Koda!" Owl commanded. "This man and this boy are the reasons we even stand a chance against that!" As Owl pointed to the waterway. The animals separated, and through the branches of the trees Koda could see the oil tanker in the waterway.

"What is that?" Koda demanded.

"We have a problem," Owl said. "As you can see, that oil tanker has run aground, and is leaking oil. Max and his grandfather have made a call to a man who is coming to help us."

"A MAN? MORE HUMANS?" Koda bellowed, angry and not knowing what to think.

"Yes, Koda," Tonkawa jumped in. "This is what I was trying to tell you. We can no longer live without working with the humans. There are many humans who will help us and ask for nothing in return."

Koda looked at Tonkawa, and as he did, his eyes softened and his body eased from the tension that had built up. Breathing deeply, Koda could see where his thinking could have gotten everyone killed. Koda began, "Tonkawa, I look at you and see a young cub, and I thought, how could this young cub know anything? But, you my little friend have shown this old bear how narrow minded I have been thinking." Koda walked over to Tonkawa, picked him up, and hugged him. "I hope you can forgive me. I thought I was protecting us all and our home, but I see I was only putting us all in danger by living from old fears."

Placing Tonkawa back down, Koda walked over to Max and his grandfather. "Max, Grandfather," Koda began, "thank you for caring and showing us that not all humans are unpredictable and dangerous. I can see now that we do need your help, and if we work together we come in commonality with the environment that sustains us."

Hearing the roar of engines, they looked up and saw a large plane come soaring over the mountain. "Look everyone!" Max exclaimed, pointing at it. "That's the Fungi Perfecti Mycotransport Plane!" He could tell by the markings on the side of the plane. "They are starting to come!"

All the animals cheered with excitement!

"Pablo, this is FPM, come in. Over…" Captain Owen Marshall released the radio button waiting for Pablo's reply. Not hearing a reply, Captain Owen tried again. "This is FPM approaching Hartley Bay Airport. Pablo, are you there? Over." Captains Owen and Reid thought it was very strange that Pablo didn't respond.

"We'd better take her in, Owen," Captain Reid suggested. "We need to get this bird on the ground and unloaded. I'm sure Pablo is busy with other matters concerning this cleanup effort."

"Yes, I'm sure you're right," Captain Owen agreed. With the airport in front of them, they flew the FPM plane down low and glided across the water's surface. All the animals watched in amazement. They had never seen such a large plane land on the water before.

Landing safely, the FPM plane taxied up to the docks of the Hartley Bay Airport. They had made it.

"It always seems impossible
until it's done.

Chapter Twenty-one

IT'S GOING TO TAKE MORE THAN SCIENCE

"You never told me what the process is you developed. How exactly do mushrooms help with oil spills?" Trevon asked, more intrigued by Pablo than any scientist he'd had the privilege of guiding before.

"Oh sure, let me explain," Pablo began. "We take twenty-foot hemp sacks and we stuff them full of straw. We now have twenty-foot booms. We then inject these booms with the mycelium of the Oyster mushroom. The straw becomes a food source for mushrooms. Over a few weeks the mycelium consumes the straw and then we have twenty-foot Mycobooms. We then take these Mycobooms and put them into the oil spill. The Mycobooms float and suck up the oil and breaks it down into a simple sugar. The oil dissolves."

"You have got to be kidding me. These mushrooms eat oil?" Trevon asked in disbelief.

"No, not exactly eat oil, they break it down into a simple sugar and the oil dissolves, but that's not all. What happens next is simply remarkable," Pablo said with a smile on his face.

"More remarkable than mushrooms breaking down oil? Okay, I'm listening," Trevon replied, thinking the story sounded too fantastical.

"The Oyster Mushroom then sprouts fruiting bodies, and they grow out of the sides of the bags. They drop their spores, and this attracts flies. The flies then attract trout and the circle of life can begin again. A healthy ecosystem is restored," Pablo explained. "But, it takes more than science Trevon. It takes people taking action."

"So, you are going to take these Mycobooms and drop them into this oil spill?" Trevon asked.

"That's the plan, but I have to tell you, it's exactly what we have been doing and studying for several years. This time we are just doing it on a much larger scale."

"Larger scale? I guess it's a larger scale, Pablo. This is amazing!" Trevon felt excited, because he understood what this could mean for the environment and the wildlife–for the planet.

"Look Pablo," Trevon said. "There it is, the Hartley Bay Airport. We're here!"

"It looks like the boys made it, too, with the Fungi Perfecti Mycotransport. Very good!" Pablo pointed to the plane beside the dock.

"That's your plane?" Trevon asked.

"Yes, that's the plane we use to service the oil spills. It can carry the Mycobooms to remote areas like this one. It has made all the difference in helping us clean up these spills. I'm afraid that without it, we wouldn't be as nearly as effective as we are," Pablo replied. "And wait until you see what is waiting for us to help deploy these Mycobooms!"

"Sounds exciting! Let's get you over there." Trevon accelerated his riverboat and quickly pulled up to the docks of the airport.

With hugs all around, Captains Owen and Reid greeted Pablo as he came off the docks.

"Imagination will often carry us to worlds that never were, but without it we go nowhere.

Carl Sagan

Chapter Twenty-two

CALLING ALL HIS CHILDREN HOME

"Hello, boys," Pablo said. "It's so good to see you! How was your flight?"

"No problems at all, and look, we even unloaded all the Mycobooms," Captain Reid said as he pointed to the Mycobooms stacked on the tarmac.

Looking beyond the booms and to the large hanger just beyond, Pablo could see the Erickson Aircrane. "Well look at that, Andy delivered," Pablo said with relief, but not surprised.

"Yes, sir," Captain Owen said. "And Captain LaDena just arrived. She's still in the Erickson."

"Captain Ladena?" Pablo said with a smile. "Andy said she would be piloting for us."

"Oh yes, Pablo," Captain Owen began. "She's more than a pilot—she was telling us how she flies that big bird into some dangerous situations. Forest fires, rock slides, landslides, you name it and she's done it!

"Did she tell you about the time she flew into a molten lava flow in Hawaii?" Pablo asked. He grinned as he watched Trevon and the Captains look at each other in disbelief. "That's right! She airlifted a hundred people off the roof of a building that was in direct path of a lava flow!"

"No kidding!" Trevon exclaimed.

"Well, let's go see what she thinks of oil spills," Pablo replied and walked over to the helicopter.

"Hello, Dad!," Captain LaDena said as she opened the helicopter door, jumped down, and ran up to Pablo. She gave him a big hug.

"So good to see you too, LeDena. Andy told me you were up here fighting few forest fires. Everything under control?"

"Oh sure, Dad! It was a lot of work and it was touch and go there for a while, but we were able to stop them before they got out of control," LeDena replied. "As soon as Andy put the call out and explained what was going on, I asked for the assignment."

"I am not surprised, thank you."

Pablo turned to the others. "Fellas, let me introduce you to my daughter."

Everyone stood there speechless, looking at each other. They had no idea that Captain LeDena was Pablo's daughter.

Smiling, Pablo said, "Well, we need to get a plan together, so let's go see what we are dealing with. Trevon, I need you take me over to that cliff," Pablo pointed to the shore line just beyond the tanker. "I need to get a better look at the tanker and the oil spill."

"Yes sir," Trevon replied, eager to help in any way he could. LeDena and Trevon both felt something stirring deep inside of them that motivated them to help as it was part of their ancestral heritage.

Pulling up to the shore, Pablo got out of the boat and walked up to the top of the cliff. Standing and overlooking the tanker, now completely on its side,

Pablo assessed the situation. Reaching for his phone, he called the National Oceanic and Atmospheric Administration Service.

"Hello, this Paul Stamets. Could you connect me to someone in Tides and Currents, please?"

"Yes sir, can you please hold?" the operator asked.

A moment later, Pablo heard, "Yes, this is the Tides and Currents department, how may I help you?"

"Hello, I am here at Hartley Bay and I need the tide table for this area. I was hoping you could give me the tide table for Hartley Bay, B.C. Canada?"

"Yes sir," said the voice from NOAA. "Low tide is 12:30 pm running 4.7 feet and high tide will be at 7:31 pm running at 17.6 feet."

"Okay, thank you for your help," Pablo replied, putting away his phone. He walked back down to the shore where Trevon was waiting. "Okay, Trevon, I've seen enough. Let's head back."

Pulling up to the dock, he could see the crew waiting to hear what Pablo wanted to do next.

"Looks like high tide will be at 7:31 pm," Pablo said. "It's now 3:00 pm. Folks, we only have four hours to get that oil under control."

"What's the plan?" LaDena asked.

"First, we need to daisy chain together about two-hundred Mycobooms and stack them down on the shore. LaDena, do you have a way of dropping one Mycoboom at a time?" Pablo asked.

"Sure, thing Pablo, I can use the Heli-Claw. I can operate it by remote control. It gives me pinpoint accuracy for picking up and unloading supplies," replied LaDena.

"I will need you to pick up the remaining 160 Mycobooms and I will tell you where to drop them," Pablo said.

"What about the daisy-chained Mycobooms? How are you going to get those out into the water?" Captain Owen asked.

"Not to worry," Pablo replied as he looked at his watch. Just then, a large tug boat sounded its horn. "Right on time," Pablo said. "Excuse me for minute, I need to go meet an old friend."

"What in the name...?" Trevon could not believe what he was seeing.

The big tug pulled up to the dock and was secured by the crew. The captain of the tug boat came walking up to greet Pablo.

"You're right on time!" said Pablo as he hugged the captain.

"Is there anyone he doesn't know?" Trevon asked.

"Tug Boat Captain Betsy!" Pablo introduced her to the group. "It's been too long." "Pablo, it is so good to see you," Captain Betsy began, " but I'm sorry it's

under these circumstances. Once you called, I got my crew together and headed right out. I now understand the urgency. What a mess, huh?"

"I knew I could count on you," Pablo replied. "Yes, we have a real emergency on our hands. We are under a time crunch. We only have four hours to contain that oil spill." Pablo turned and pointed at the listing tanker.

"Just tell me what you need us to do Pablo, we're ready," Captain Betsy said confidently.

"We need to get those Mycobooms onto your Tug." Pablo replied.

"How many do you have there?" Betsy asked.

"There are two hundred, and we need to daisy chain them together as we drop them into the water. We can connect them on the tug as you move it around the perimeter of the oil spill. You think your crew can handle that okay?" Pablo asked.

"This crew?" Betsy answered. "I trust this crew with my life! We won't let you down. Crew!" Betsy yelled out. "We need those Mycobooms on the tug." Instantly the crew moved into action, and in less than half an hour the booms were loaded and ready to go.

With the booms secured on the tug boat, Pablo headed back to give direction to LaDena.

"LaDena, I will need to fly with you, so I can make sure the oil spill is being effectively corralled. We can't have any leak through on this one."

"Not a problem, Pablo. Let's get those Mycobooms tucked under the belly of the Erickson," Ladena said.

"How can we help?" Trevon asked.
"Trevon, have you ever operated a forklift before?" Pablo asked.

"Yes, actually I have. On my father's farm, I used to move the hay bales and load them on the flatbeds."

"Perfect," Pablo said encouraged. "I knew there was more to our meeting than you giving me a ride up river."

Trevon smiled, feeling excited and proud that he could continue to play a role in this critical effort.

"Captain Reid and Owen let's get to the Erickson so when Trevon brings up those Mycobooms we can help get them loaded up."

Pablo directed every aspect of this effort like a conductor of a large orchestra. Without a plan the wildlife and ecosystems wouldn't stand a chance.

"We are like butterflies
that flutter for a day
and think it is forever.

Carl Sagan

Chapter Twenty-three

HOPEFULLY, THE SPIRIT
OF GOODNESS WILL SURVIVE

By now, all the animals of the forest had heard about the oil spill. There were animals lining the shore. The trees were filled every kind of bird, and up on the cliff, Max, Grandpa, Tonkawa, Taru, and the others stood anxiously watching all the action on the other side of the river.

"What's going on?" Koda asked.

"Looks to me like Pablo is directing the rescue effort," Grandpa began. "That tug boat is loaded with those Mycobooms, and see that giant helicopter? Well, if I had to guess, that must be how he plans on dropping them into that oil spill."

"Get out of town," Wolverine said in disbelief.

"I'd say Grandpa is right," Max replied.

"Well if they can move all those boomy things around that oil, I'll be a monkey's uncle." Wolverine said, smiling.

"Monkey? What's a monkey?" Tonkawa asked. Everyone stopped and for a moment just stared at Tonkawa. Then, all at once, everyone started to laugh.

"Look, everyone!" Max said, pointing to the tug moving towards the oil spill. "And look, that helicopter is in the air, too!"

It had started. The effort to secure the oil spill was underway. All the animals of Gribbell Island stood in awe and anxiously watched as the humans worked to save their home.

Meanwhile, the marine engineers arrived at the tanker. Their job was to get

to the hole in the tanker and close it up. As they worked, Pablo and his team went to work.

"I never would have believed it if I didn't see this with my own eyes," Koda said, staring in disbelief.

"Yeah, we know," Taru said. Koda and Taru looked at each other from the corner of their eyes and smiled.

The tug boat moved around the outside of the oil spill, dropping a Mycoboom every twenty feet. Captain Betsy had her crew working as one and they moved quickly and accurately around the oil spill.

Meanwhile, Pablo was watching the progress from the Erickson. The tug closed the loop on the oil spill. The oil spill was contained. The tug's horn sounded so loudly that all the animals could hear it. The animals could see that the oil spill had Mycobooms all around it, and all at once, they cheered!

"Now for the final phase, LaDena. Let's drop these inside the spill." Pablo motioned to LaDena to get closer to the water. "We have one hour. Do you think we can get these booms dropped within that time?"

"Not a problem, Dad," LaDena reassured her father. "These booms are very light compared to some of the things I've had to move, and this Heli-Claw is truly an amazing piece of equipment."

Pablo couldn't believe how LaDena could fly the Erickson and operate the Heli-Claw at the same time, and with such accuracy. Pablo understood how she had gained her reputation. Within forty-five minutes, LaDena had the booms spread throughout the oil spill.

The animals watched the giant helicopter fly over the spill placing booms throughout the oil spill. All the animals stood amazed at what the humans had accomplished for them.

They watched as the tug and helicopter made their way back to the docks to Hartley Bay airport.

Standing on the tarmac of the airport, the whole team cheered and congratulated one another.

"How do I even begin to thank you all?" Pablo began. "My friends, without each and every one of you, this would not have been possible. I cannot thank you enough. The significance of the many ecosystems you saved today, the wildlife, the marine life, birds, plants and trees that make the Great Bear Rainforest their home cannot be overstated. It is to all of them that we are honored to serve them. It is they who contribute to the natural beauty of this region."

Pablo had noticed the animals on the cliff across the river the whole time the effort was underway. Walking over to Trevon Pablo asked, "Trevon, how about you give me one last ride in your boat?"'

"Of course, Pablo! Where do you want to go?" Trevon asked, leading Pablo to his riverboat.

"See that cliff over there that breaks into the clearing? Let's take a drive over there." Pablo replied.

"You got it!" Trevon steered his riverboat to the other side of the river. "You know, Pablo, if you had told me this morning this was how I was going to spend my day I never would have believed you. I will never forget this day as long as I live."

"Well hang on, Trevon, I don't think this river is done with us quite yet."

As they neared the shore, Trevon jumped out and pulled his boat up on the beach. "Okay, what's next?"

Just as Trevon finished his question, animals of all kinds started coming out of the woods. At first Trevon was nervous. "What's going on? Are you seeing this?"

"Just remain calm, Trevon. These animals won't hurt us," Pablo said with a certainty that instantly made Trevon feel safe.

As the animals kept coming from the forest, they parted to reveal Max walking with Tonkawa. Behind them came Grandpa and Taru, then Koda, Wolverine, and Wolf. Finally, Owl came gliding in and landed on Trevon's shoulder.

"Pablo?" Trevon said nervously, holding perfectly still.

"Just relax, everything is okay," Pablo said reassuringly. Once again, Trevon felt calm and safe.

"You must be Max," Pablo began. "And you must be Grandpa. I am so glad to finally meet you."

"Meet us?" Grandpa said, surprised. "We are glad to meet you!"

"I don't think you fully understand what you two have accomplished!" Pablo exclaimed. "You started last year by calling me about the bees, and because you did, look at what you accomplished. Now, this. Look around you. Do you see?"

Max and Grandpa stood in silence and looked at the animals that were surrounding them. Max looked at Tonkawa and realized how fortunate he was to make friends with such a rare and beautiful animal. He then looked at Taru and then to Koda and the magnificence of these bears set him back a step. The gratitude struck deep into the hearts of Max and Grandpa.

Bending down to look at Max in his eyes, Pablo whispered, "Don't forget this moment, Max."

Pablo walked over to Taru and Koda to show respect to Tonkawa's mother and to the leader of the bear clan.

Koda stood dumbfounded by this human. What Koda had witnessed today, he thought was impossible. Koda stepped forward and began, "Animals of the forest, hear me now. You all know our old—and tired—rules of forbidding any contact with humans." Looking down at Tonkawa. "A very wise bear once told me that we can no longer survive in this world without learning to work with humans, but I was too stubborn to listen. I want you all to know that if it wasn't for Tonkawa and his friend Max, this day would have turned out very differently. But, it didn't turn out that way, did it?" A loud cheer from everyone went up.

"No, indeed it did not," Taru replied with a proud smile on her face, for her cub and his friend Max.

"Let today mark the changes we now make forever. For the survival of all of us who live with the spirit of nature in our hearts," Koda said as he nodded respectfully to Pablo.

Pablo, bringing his hands together, bowed to Koda.

Max looked around at the animals that had gathered, and then he looked out to the tanker and the men working on her. "Pablo, a disaster was avoided here today, thanks to you."

Pablo looked at Max and Tonkawa. "It does takes a team, but it is you we have to thank, Max. It took a lot of courage. You ventured off on a journey into this vast wilderness with wonder. You have seen first firsthand how these living creatures are locked in the daily challenge of survival. When things looked like all was lost, you didn't panic—you knew you had to do something. With what you have learned here, you can create awareness."

Standing among the animals, Pablo continued, "I want you to know that I believe nature is a force for good. Good is not only concept, it is a spirit—it's one that both humans and animals can share—and so hopefully the spirit of goodness will survive."

More About The Great Bear Rainforest

Canada is home to one of the most unspoiled and complicated ecosystems in the world. It is also home to one of the most unique creatures found on Earth, what the Gitga'at First Nation people call mooksgm'ol, the Spirit Bear (also known as the Kermode bear). It is a North American black bear with creamy white fur.

With less than four hundred remaining, the spirit bear lives in one place on Earth, The Great Bear Rainforest on British Columbia's coast. The Great Bear Rainforest is the largest temperate rainforest in the world. Once upon a time, this rare coastal ecosystem covered sixty million acres that stretched from Northern California to Alaska. Today, over half of the original forest has been logged. What makes matters worse is that in California, Oregon, and Washington states, large-scale forest conservation can no longer be an option (ref. Rainforest Solution Project).

Coastal temperate rainforest sustains more biomass than any other terrestrial ecosystem on Earth, including black bears, Kermode bears, grizzlies, wolves and six million migratory birds (ref. Rainforest Solution Project). All six species of Pacific Salmon spawn in the regions maze of rivers, fjords, channels and streams (ref. Sierra Club of British Columbia). Three thousand genetically distinct salmon stocks are increasingly becoming endangered (ref. Rainforest Solution Project).

Regardless of the signed agreements dating back as far 2001, clear-cut logging continues in the Great Bear Rainforest. Eighty percent of the Rainforest valleys in BC have been cut and destroyed (ref. Greenpeace), which makes it increasingly difficult for the grey wolf. They too live on the Great Bear Rainforest and are genetically unique and distinct from all other wolves in Canada (ref. Rainforest Solution Project).

What will it take to create a paradigm shift in our thinking? The challenge before us is finding new ways to live in harmony with nature and invent a new path of knowledge. How do we inspire the youth to become citizen scientists? Ask yourself: what can I do to help create positive change?

In this world today, there are examples of individuals who asked that very question and came up with creative and innovative answers; their work is seen and written about in this book. Because of them, this book exists.

"In the end,
there is always
a new beginning.

David Marshall

Made in the USA
Las Vegas, NV
18 February 2022